EVEN THE STUBBORN FALL...

BEND

VEGAS HEAT - BOOK ONE

USA TODAY BESTSELLING AUTHOR

MOLLY McLAIN

Bend (Vegas Heat—Book One)
Published by Molly McLain Books, LLC
Copyright © 2016 Molly McLain Books, LLC

Cover Design:
Designs by Dana

Cover Photo:
Licensed through DepositPhotos

Editor:
Ellie McLove

Interior Book Design & Formatting:
Christine Borgford, Type A Formatting

BEND

Amy,
Best. Bathroom.
Fuck. Ever.

♡

Molly
McLain

To Maline & Trisha, my Vegas partners in crime.
Can't wait to do it again, ladies!

CHAPTER One

Trent

"YOU'RE KIDDING ME." The pretty brunette blinks up at me from the driver's side window, her copper eyes as big and as bright as the Las Vegas sun.

"Afraid not, ma'am. License, registration, and insurance?" I ask again, this time holding out my hand. She thinks she'll get special treatment because she's the captain's daughter? Not on my watch, babe.

"Don't be a dick, Trent. I'm already late for work."

And yet she makes no move for the paperwork I've asked for. Twice.

"Ma'am, I'm going to ask you one more time for your license, registration, and insurance. If you fail to cooperate, I'll be forced to call for backup, at which time you'll be escorted from your vehicle." Looks like she's wearing a short skirt this morning. Might be a nice start to my day.

"Goddammit, Trent! I seriously don't have time for this shit!"

Neither do I, but Kinsey with her panties in a bunch is a show I'd hate to miss. "Then I suggest you do as I ask, Ms. Malloy."

She narrows those fiery eyes at me before she gives an exasperated huff and reaches for her purse. "Do you enjoy being a jerk, *Sergeant Clark?*"

As a matter of fact, I do. Especially when she's involved. It's nothing personal—it's just fun.

"You know damn well I'm valid on both accounts, since you just pulled me over *last week.*"

"A lot could change in seven days, ma'am."

"Ugh!" she groans, snatching her license from her wallet. "Quit with the *ma'am* crap already! I'm younger than you, for God's sake!"

Probably explains why she can't drive for shit. "You do realize that this is the very same location I pulled you over the other day, do you not, Ms. Malloy?"

She shoves her information at me and rolls her eyes. "How could I forget?"

"You're aware that I could revoke your license as a repeat offender?" I inspect her ID, admiring the pretty smile on her face. She's a friggin' knockout when she's not chewing my ass.

"You wouldn't do that," she sneers, her cherry lips turned up into the slightest of smiles. "Because then you'd have no one to harass."

"Not harassing you, ma'am. Just doing my job. A job you secure a little more every time you disobey the traffic sign and turn right on red."

With a soft snort, she crosses her arms over her chest and looks ahead, where the Vegas strip is just starting to wake up. Not that it ever really slept.

"All right, Ms. Malloy . . ." I hand her information back through the window, as my radio squawks in my ear. A DOA in a hotel room just down the block. "I'll let you off with another warning just because I've got shit to do. You won't be so lucky next time."

"Don't worry—there won't be a next time."

Yeah, there will. I'll make sure of it. "Have a nice day, Ms. Malloy."

"Fuck you, Trent."

I laugh as she puts her little red Audi into drive and pulls away. Someone needs to teach that girl some manners.

Guess it'll have to be me.

Kinsey

"YOU GOT PULLED over again?" Jana's mouth drops open behind the counter, where she preps the cash register for the day.

"I swear he has it out for me," I grumble, still just as pissed now, as I was when I saw the cocky bastard step out of his SUV. Again. "Maybe I should talk to my dad."

"And tell him what? You ran a red light?"

"I stopped!" I just went again when the coast was clear.

Jana smirks as I grab the mail from the basket and rifle through it, only half paying attention. I can't stop seeing Sergeant Hardass approach my car, one long, arrogant step after the other. That dark hair whipping in the morning breeze. Those stupid aviator sunglasses making him look like an 80's sitcom knock-off. Those big, muscled forearms that made me squirm in my seat, not once, but *twice* in the past week.

"I hate him," I mutter, tucking the envelopes under one arm so I can carry my coffee and purse back to my office with the other. "He's probably one of those guys with a big ego and a little dick."

"Or he's hung and he knows it."

"So not helping, Jan."

She laughs while I head to the back of the store, past the bins of panties and headless mannequins wearing this season's latest in intimate apparel. "Tally should be here in an hour," I call over my shoulder. "Let me know if she's late."

"Will do, boss lady."

For the next twenty minutes, I submerge myself in the hundred or so unanswered emails in my inbox. It's my usual morning routine, as the manager of Chloe's Closet, one of Vegas's high-end lingerie stores, and today it proves to be the perfect distraction from the shitty start to my day.

Until I see the email from my father.

You remember the PD ball is coming up, right? Would love for you to be my date.

Ugh. At every single PD event, he tries to marry me off to Will Vaccaro. Even when Will was engaged to someone else, the poor guy.

I close the message without responding, and move on. The next is from the Miracle Mile's Head of Security.

Morning, Kins. Took a look at the surveillance from last week. We should talk.

Crap, I was afraid he'd say that.

Hitting his number on speed dial, I keep a close eye on my open door. Tipping off my employees is the last freaking thing I need today.

"Hey, Mick, it's Kinsey. Whatchya got?"

The older man's heavy, out-of-shape sigh crackles the line. "You're not gonna like it, Toots."

"I guessed as much. How bad?"

"It's hard to say, but I'm almost positive she's up to something. Either that, or she's got early onset Alzheimer's, because she's in and out of the store at least three times every night at closing."

Shit. "Is she taking anything with her?"

"Just her purse, but she's gone enough between trips that it's possible she's emptying it out between trips."

Like the trunk of her car, maybe. Where she's set up her own bra and panty shop, because I can't imagine why anyone would need as much lingerie as she's taken if they weren't selling it on the side.

"Get your cameras fixed, Kins. Then we'll know for sure what's going on."

About that . . ."Can't you look at them? You're the security guru."

"I'll take that as a compliment, but Ben's the one who fixes things. You know that."

Yes, but Ben Sully's interest in fixing things ends at the end of the Miracle Mile. It does not, however, stretch to relationships or shitty sex. "Fine," I sigh. "But he probably won't call me back."

"Come on, sweet cheeks, you're as nice as pie. Who wouldn't want to call you back?"

"My ex?"

"Minor technicality," Mick chuckles. "Just let me know if he accidentally deletes your message. I'll get on him."

I roll my eyes and sip my coffee. "Thanks, Micky. Tell Margo I said hi."

"Will do. Hey, you might want to call the PD, too. See what they have to say. I'm happy to share my footage if they want it."

Ick. I respect my father's profession, but I'd prefer to avoid the police. Especially when they pull me over for complete bullshit reasons. Also because Dad will try to throw his weight around and make me feel like a little girl in front of his men.

"We'll see." Blowing a kiss, I hang up. I've already run the numbers and the inventory doesn't match up. Just like last week, and the week before. Heck, the last month. There's only one common denominator, and Mick just confirmed she's been acting suspicious on camera. Aside from catching her red handed—which I'd prefer not to do myself, given her hot temper—I only have two options . . .

Fix the freakin' cameras or call the cops. Both are going to suck, but one might suck just a little less than the other, so I pick up the phone and dial.

Trent

"NOT MY JOB, man." I shake my head and continue searching the DOA's hotel room for anything out of the ordinary. It's hard to say what that might be, however, considering the guy must've partied pretty hard before he went down. Empty bottles of booze are scattered across every surface, and I've already bagged four used condoms.

"This isn't your job, either." My buddy, Will, smirks. "Yet you're digging in just fine."

"I like this shit."

"Hanging out with bloated bodies? You're one sick fuck, Clark."

I toss one of the sealed condom bags at him and he catches it in one hand, while flipping me off with the other. I grin. "I'm pretty sure Malloy told you to go, anyway, seeing as you're his favorite and he's betting on you calling him Pops someday."

Will's face turns as red as the blood-stained sheets beneath our vic. "Shut the fuck up."

"What?" I laugh. "You pretty much have his blessing to date the princess, so why not?"

"Because it's a fucking trap!" He shakes his head, and then makes a mocking face. *"Go ahead, Detective. Ask her out. Then, for shits and giggles, I'll track your ass down and neuter you like the dog you are."*

"She's wearing a nice skirt today. Might be worth it." I shrug and bag what looks like a wad of chewing tobacco. Might also be shit, but I'm hoping for the former.

"When the hell did you see her?"

"Pulled her over this morning."

"Didn't you just do that last week?"

"Yep." I seal the bag and toss it over to one of the techs for labeling. "Apparently, she doesn't think the law applies to her."

"That or you're a prick."

Well, that would be shocking, wouldn't it? Me . . . a prick. I sure as hell didn't get where I am being Mr. Fucking Nice Guy. "If the shoe fits."

Will shakes his head and checks his watch. "I told Captain we'd head over to the Mile right away. It's been four minutes. He's probably written both of us up by now."

"Better get your ass moving then." I've had enough of Kinsey Malloy and her *my-shit-don't-stink* attitude for one day.

"Hey, Will, you worked the Flamingo DOA last week, didn't you?" one of the other detectives calls from beside the body. "You wanna come check this out?"

My buddy flashes a grin. "Guess the princess is all yours."

Fucking bastard.

Kinsey

"IS THIS SOME kind of joke?" I blink at the man who enters the coffee shop on the other side of the Miracle Mile, where hopefully none of my employees spots me talking to the police. Or in this case, Sergeant Hardass.

"I friggin' wish," he grumbles, and drops into the chair across from me with a huff. "Apparently, I'm a jack of all trades today."

"You mean, jackass of all trades, don't you?" I watch him carefully as he pulls off the sunglasses and runs a hand through his hair. Damn, those blue eyes are nice without the shades.

"Funny lady." Waving over the waitress, he orders a tall Americano with a double shot. "Didn't know you had a sense of humor."

"Oh, I'm hella funny. When I'm not being targeted by a cop who obviously has nothing better to do with his time."

He swings those intense eyes back to me, one eyebrow arched. "I'll have you know I just left a major crime scene."

"You're not supposed to tell me that. It's a breach of confidentiality."

He grunts. "Like you count."

"Damn right I count. In fact, right now, I'm a concerned citizen with a potential criminal complaint. Shouldn't you be treating me a little better?"

"You know," he begins, leaning those thick, muscled arms on the table between us. "I seem to recall a certain citizen telling me to fuck off this morning."

Yeah, well, he deserved it. "What's your point?"

"This respect thing goes both ways, princess."

"Princess?" I smirk. It's my dad's pet name for me; unfortunately every guy in the Metro has caught on. "Don't let my daddy hear you say that."

Those baby blues glaze over with something I can't quite put my finger on before his mouth curls up into a lopsided smile. He's one of those men with a lush bottom lip that most women would kill for. The long eyelashes, too. Bastard. "How about we just cut to the chase and you tell me what you called the PD for."

"I think someone's stealing from the store."

"Oh, shit. A panty pilferer. Call the fucking FBI."

My face goes instantly hot and suddenly calling my ex-boy-friend seems a lot more appealing. "Fuck you, Trent," I say for the second time today, as I grab my coffee and inventory-tracking folder he's apparently not interested in looking at.

"Come on, Kinsey, I'm just giving you shit."

Yeah, well, screw that. I'll take care of this problem by my-self, just like I do everything else.

CHAPTER Two

Trent

"YOU BRINGING A date to the shindig this weekend?" Dez asks, as I push my last two-fifty toward his ready hands.

"Fuck, no," I grunt, but not because of the exertion. "You know I don't do black tie." Or dates, for that matter.

He shakes his head and helps me put the bar back on the rails. "Captain's gonna have your ass, missing the ball three years in a row."

Like I give a shit. I joined the PD to kick ass and keep assholes off the streets, not to fucking waltz. "Oh, well," I say, curling upright and brushing off my hands. "Won't be the first time, and surely won't be the last."

"How'd the interview with the princess go yesterday?" Will saunters over and drops to the bench when I get up.

"Like shit." The woman's either got a serious stick up her ass or she's never been fucked properly. If I had my guess, I'd say she suffers from a little of both. "She flipped out on me like she always does."

"Well, quit pulling her over then," Dez chuckles, and I grin.

"Not my fault she can't follow the law."

Will smirks as he powders his hands. "If I didn't know better, I'd say you had a thing for *Miss Thang*, Clark."

Fuck that shit. I like the mouths on my women to be doing

something other than bitching. "Nah, man, she's all yours."

Dez snickers at the head of the bench. "I heard she's the captain's date this weekend. Maybe you'll get lucky and score a dance, man."

Will's face turns red before he even touches the bar. "You guys know that shit ain't funny."

"Oh, but it is." Will's not a saint by any means, but he's the best option the captain's got for his little girl. The only one of us who's ever even tried a serious relationship. "In fact, maybe you should just give it up already. Take her out. Hell, buy the damn ring."

Dez's eyes go wide as soon as the words leave my mouth, but I don't care. Maybe twisting the knife that's still stuck in my buddy's side is what he needs. Coddling his sorry ass sure hasn't helped.

Will's hands ball into fists at his sides, then he rolls upright with a venomous scowl. "You know what? Fuck you, Clark. At least I tried with a woman."

I snort. "Is that supposed to hurt my feelings? Because I'm perfectly happy just the way things are." Free and easy. Not a commitment in sight.

"That's because you don't know any better." His dark eyes narrow. "*Suck me, fuck me.* That's your motto, right? Have you ever even spent the night with a woman? You know, without skipping out at two in the morning with your tail between your legs?"

"This guy," I laugh, looking at Dez. "Give him a little shit and he festers right up."

"You just wait." Will's scowl morphs into a smug grin. "One of these days, some pretty little thing is gonna knock your cocky ass right to the ground."

Fat fucking chance. I know better than to get roped into that shit. Unlike him.

"Whatever." I wave him off and grab my towel. "You two have fun planning for your prissy little dance this weekend. I'm gonna go clean up the streets."

I don't wait for either of them to come back with another jab. Why? I don't live my life around other people. I do me before anyone else, aside from when I'm wearing my badge. Maybe it makes me an asshole, but that's how I roll. Take it or leave it.

Kinsey

TWO WEEKS INTO the month and we're already down almost two grand in missing inventory. That's more than all of last quarter combined, and if I don't come up with some kind of explanation, headquarters is going to have my butt in a sling.

Pushing aside the figures, I grab my phone. Ben or my dad directly? Both feel like I'd be giving away a little piece of my soul and, right now, with Chloe's bottom line slowly dying, I need to preserve all the humility I can.

"Ugh, this sucks," I groan to myself, thumbing the phone on and scrolling to my contacts. Not to mention, if I call Dad, he's going to want an answer about the ball. It isn't that I mind going with him—I love spending time with him—it's just the company he keeps.

Trent Clark, case in point.

My thumb hovers over Ben's name for a solid thirty seconds before I click on it and cringe the entire time the phone rings in my ear.

"Never thought I'd see your name on my caller ID again," that familiar male voice sneers in the phone by way of greeting.

I pinch my eyes shut and take a deep breath. I never thought he'd actually answer. "Hey, Ben. How are you?"

"Pretty shitty according to you, but maybe you've forgotten."

Ugh. I'm such a horrible person. "Ben, you know I didn't mean to hurt your feelings."

"Eh." He sighs through the phone. "Doesn't really matter now, does it? You've moved on, I've moved on . . ."

He has?

"You knew that though, right? I assume that's why you're calling."

Um . . ."Actually, no."

His laugh is low and smarmy. Kind of slimy, if I'm honest.

"Tally didn't tell you?"

Tally? How could he possibly know I'm calling about her?

"I've been seeing her for a month now," he goes on. "Gotta tell ya, Kins—she hasn't complained once about the way I fuck."

Oh. My. God. "You're kidding me, right?"

He laughs again. "You know, maybe you being a greedy, stuck up bitch actually worked to my advantage. Not only did you walk, but you opened my eyes to—"

Click. I end the call and drop the phone onto my desk.

You are not an awful person, Kinsey. You only told him the truth. A truth you thought he could handle, six months into your relationship. Your comfortable, albeit less than orgasmic, relationship.

And now he's screwing Tally. Could this possibly be any more messed up?

"Knock, knock . . ." Jana ducks her head into my office with a big, goofy grin on her face. "Thought you should know that there's a big, beefy cop at the register asking to speak with you."

"My dad?"

Jana's face sours like I just force-fed her cat food. "Oh, my God, no. Eww."

"Eww?" Clearly the conversation with Ben has screwed up my ability to comprehend.

"I was just going to ask if he's the one who's packing in the pants, but now you've ruined my fantasy. And made me a little queasy, too."

"Trent is here?" I push to my feet in a rush. No one can know I'm talking to the police about the missing stock. "Um . . ." Think, Kinsey, think. "Do I, uh, look okay?" I ask, patting at my hair, and going with the first thing that comes to mind: Pretend that Trent Clark isn't here on official police business.

Jana's eyes brighten once again. "You look freakin' amazing." Then she squeals. "See, I knew this would happen."

"You knew what would happen?" I ask dumbly. Again, the brain just isn't functioning like it should be apparently. Freaking Ben.

"You and the hot cop. Now I get why he kept pulling you over!"

Oh, no. No, no, no. There isn't a single spark between Sergeant Hardass and me. You know, other than he's sexy as crap. But that's just bad boy fantasy stuff. In real life, I can't stand him.

"Can you send him back here, please?" I ask, feigning what I hope looks like a nervous, girly smile.

Jana nods eagerly, then disappears, leaving me to absolutely panic. Tally isn't working today, right? And other than Jana, I have Samantha on the floor. Between the two of them, the entire Mile will think I'm banging a Metro cop by the time he actually leaves. Um . . . okay. It's only marginally better than the truth, but a little better is better than no better.

"Thanks, Jana," Trent's low chuckle carries down the hall a second before he appears in my doorway with a shit-eating grin on his face. He meets my eye, then not-so-discreetly glances back down the hall. Presumably at my best employee's ass.

"You're such a pig," I sneer, hurrying around the desk to close the door behind him. "And what the hell are you doing here, anyway?"

"I have an interview to finish," he says casually, making his way to a poster on my wall. The new fall line displayed on Chloe's top models. I find it motivational, though I'm sure his interest is much less refined.

"I told you yesterday that I was no longer interested in speaking with you," I say firmly, trying to keep my eyes above his shoulders, which makes me no better than him at the moment, but he doesn't need to know that.

"Doesn't work that way, princess. If you call the police with an issue, it's my job to, at the very least, gather information about your concern."

"You can't just report that I changed my mind?"

"I could, but then it's kind of like that little boy who cried wolf, you know?" He moves from the poster to a picture of me and Dad in Florida a couple years ago. The summer we spread Mom's ashes in the ocean. "It also looks bad for me if I can't provide a more detailed report, but let's not make this about me, huh?" He flashes a bright grin, followed by a wink that sends shivers down my spine.

"How have you kept your job as long as you have?"

"Come on now, Kins. Just because my work ethic challenges your prudish take on life doesn't mean you have to hate me."

Did he just call me a prude? Seriously?

I swallow down a snappish response and lift my chin. *Get him out of here as fast as possible. Don't egg him on.* "Let's make this quick, shall we? I don't need you hanging around, drawing attention."

He shrugs and drops his big body into the chair across from mine. With his legs spread wide in those slightly snug black slacks, it's harder than ever to keep my gaze on his. And from the sparkle in his eyes, he knows it.

"So, you said something about theft yesterday?"

I nod and reclaim my seat. "The inventory doesn't match the sales. Now, we account for a certain amount of petty theft, especially since stealing personal garments can be so easy. But this damage is more significant." I slide my loss spreadsheet over to him, but he barely glances at it.

"Do you have any unusually regular customers? Someone who might be slowly swiping shit from under your nose?"

I bite my lip. "I guess I didn't think of that."

"An employee, maybe?"

I nod. "There's a girl named Tally who closes a lot. I have no concrete reason to think it's her other than my gut."

"You have cameras installed?"

My face goes warm. "Yes, but they're . . . not currently working."

"Seriously, Kins? You're the captain's kid and you don't abide by retail rule number one?"

"They went down in a storm a few months back and I just . . . never got around to fixing them." I'd been more concerned about the break-up with Ben. Sue me.

He shakes his head and sighs. "So why do you think it's her?"

"Because the daily numbers match up when she doesn't close, and they're only off when she's here. Also, the mall's main surveillance shows her coming and going from the store after she's closed up."

"Get your cameras fixed. It's as easy as that."

Except it's not. "That might take a bit."

He frowns. "Then I'm not sure what you want me to do here . . ."

"I know!" I push a hand through my hair. "It's just . . ." Ugh. "Look, I want to get the cameras fixed, but the mall's maintenance manager isn't exactly my biggest fan."

Trent blinks at me. "What, did you tell him to fuck off, too?"

"Oh, shut up."

"Maybe if you were nicer to people—"

"He's my ex, okay?"

A crooked grin kicks up one corner of the smug cop's mouth. "Well, that explains it then."

"Can we get back to the issue at hand, please?" God, this man . . .

"Fixing your cameras is part of the issue. Shouldn't security take care of that?"

I give a heavy sigh. "Yes, but the problem isn't the cameras themselves—it's something with the wiring, which is a maintenance issue. But, that aside, isn't there something else that can be done?"

"You could catch her red-handed."

"Oh, sure." I roll my eyes. "And then what?"

"Uh, call the cops?"

Obviously, he's never met Tally, whose biggest inspiration in life happens to be Rhonda Rousey.

I shuffle the papers around on my desk anxiously, and then mutter, "My luck they'd send you over."

Trent leans forward, one eyebrow cocked. "What was that, princess?"

"Nothing. Look . . ." I hate this whole situation. Especially feeling like I'm backed into a corner, not just by Ben, but by a cop who doesn't take me seriously. Unfortunately, Hardass is my best option right now. "I have an idea."

He flashes that megawatt grin again. "I'm listening."

CHAPTER Three

Trent

"DID YOU PICK up your dress blues from the cleaners yet, Sergeant Clark?"

I glance up from the endless stack of paperwork on my desk to see the captain looming above me, his arms crossed over his broad, barrel chest.

"No, sir. Sorry to say that I can't make the ball this weekend. Death in the family." Pretty sure it's the same line I used last year, but I doubt the old man remembers.

"You don't say? I sure hope it wasn't your grandmother again. Poor woman's died three times in the past five years."

Well, hell. I flash my best grin. "You got me, Captain. Truth is there really isn't a funeral. I'm actually driving out to Cali for my cousin's wedding. I didn't want to say anything . . ." I lean forward and speak in a low—but not quiet—voice, "because he's marrying Sergeant Smith's ex."

Dez's head snaps up from the desk beside mine, a pinched *what the fuck* expression on his face.

"Oh, really?" the captain chuckles. "If you'd put half as much energy into your paperwork as you do coming up with these bullshit excuses, you'd be off patrol by now. Maybe even looking at Investigations, seeing as there's an opening coming up."

No shit? "Who's leaving?"

"Afraid that's privileged information, Sergeant. It's possible an announcement will be made at the ball. Not that you'll be there to hear it." He winks and Dez laughs.

I'd have to be twelve-years-old or three sheets to the wind to buy into that ploy. "Huh. Shame about that."

The captain's eyes narrow for a moment, before he turns to Dez. "How about you and Vaccaro?"

"Wouldn't miss the ball for the world, sir." Dez gives a thumbs-up, but we all know the captain's not really asking about him, anyway. "And Will's so excited, he can't stop talking about it."

Captain Malloy's grin all but splits his ruddy face in half. "That's what I like to hear. Men who respect this job as much as I do." With that, he swings a pointed glare back to me, then walks away.

Dez starts cackling like a goddamn hen as soon as Malloy hits his office. "Poor fucking Will. Dude doesn't stand a chance."

Poor Will is right. Captain isn't going to give up until he gets what he wants, and that's his baby girl paired up with a man just like him. Someone who respects this job, which apparently isn't me, all because I refuse to dress up in a monkey suit and suck ass all night long. Pay no mind to the fact that I'm a damn good cop or that I have more motivation and initiative than ninety-five percent of the guys who work Metro. Many of whom are currently sitting around, shooting the shit and slurping coffee, rather than doing any actual work. Not that Malloy gives a shit about that.

"Kinsey's a hot little thing, though." Dez leans back in his chair, still grinning. "She's probably got a closet full of that sexy lingerie she sells, too."

Yeah, but does she have anything more than a smokin' body

to go with it? A woman can dress up in lace and garters all day long, but if she doesn't have the attitude to back it up, the effort is lost. Kinsey's got a bark, I'll give her that much, but my guess is that's all she's got.

"Don't let Will hear you talk about his woman like that," I joke—loudly—as the man himself strolls into the office in ripped up jeans, a wife-beater, and a flat-billed cap. He's working today, so he must be trying to blend in. Probably running undercover in a drug case. Or, if he's lucky, hookers.

Will flashes a toothy grin and drops a plastic bag on my desk. From the scant amount of fabric and lace and my expertise in the area of feminine delicacies, I'm guessing it's a thong.

"Look familiar?" He leans forward, palms on my desk.

"Shit, man, I'm sorry. I'll have your mom be more careful next time she's over."

Dez roars with laughter, and Will continues to smirk. "Funny, smart ass. At first I thought they were your cousin Stacy's, but then I remembered—she doesn't wear panties."

My sarcastic expression fades and I give the desk a shove. Not hard enough to knock anything over, but enough to let him know I think he's a fucker. Have since the night he took my favorite cousin's virginity, nine years ago.

"Found these in the hotel room yesterday, under the vic." He continues to glare at me, like he's expecting something. I have no idea what.

"Look, man, I know I'm a panty whisperer and all, but I can't tell you anything about these."

"Look closer, fuckwad."

"No thanks."

He rolls his eyes. "They're from Chloe's. Along with a bag full of similar shit we found stuffed in the closet."

I snort. "So maybe your dead guy had a fetish."

"Or maybe he knew a little something about merchandise

disappearing. You know, the case you're working?"

Dez slides his chair over, eyebrow cocked. "What case?"

"Don't worry about it," I snarl, before glancing back to Will. "Pretty big stretch, thinking your dead guy is in any way related to Kinsey's situation."

"Kinsey?" Dez again. "The captain's Kinsey?"

We both ignore him, and then Will finally cuts to the chase. "Since you're such an inquisitive guy, *sure*, I'll tell you what else we found." Grabbing a chair, he spins it around and straddles it in front of my desk. "The shit in the closet still had tags. One of those waist shaping things had a security sensor, too."

"Corset," Dez corrects, and this time, Will and I both turn and glare. "What?" Our friend smirks. "Just because I look sweet and innocent, doesn't mean I am."

"Ain't a damn thing innocent about your ass," I mutter before giving the plastic bag a closer look. The thong's an extra large and, Jesus fuck, there's something white and crusty on the front panel.

"Disgusting when you don't have a name to go with the jizz, isn't it?" Will makes a face and I shrug.

"Could be the vic's."

"On that note, I'm out." Dez shudders and wheels himself back to his desk.

"We'll know for sure when the labs come back," Will replies. "In the meantime, I thought you might want to know about the panty stash. Just in case it ends up being tied into your case."

My case. Like the scrap job he tossed me is anything like he does on a daily basis.

"Hey, you hear anything about someone leaving Investigation?" I ask, keeping my voice down in case the captain decides to grace us with his presence again.

Will shakes his head. "Not a thing. Why?"

"Captain dangled the golden carrot in front of him before

you came in," Dez speaks up, and Will throws his head back and laughs.

"Fucking glad I missed that!"

I throw the panties at his face and grab my coffee cup. Friggin' empty. "Don't you have someplace to be?" I grumble. Will does these little drop-ins for the sole purpose of pissing me off, I'm sure of it. He has the job I want and he rubs it in every chance he gets.

"Actually, I've gotta drop my blues off at the cleaner before I go under for the night, so yeah, I do."

I manage to keep my reaction at a grin, but Dez fails miserably at holding back a howl of laughter. "Such a suck ass!"

Will's face turns the same annoyed shade of red it always does when someone hints about him crawling up the captain's ass. Or Kinsey's ass. "Fuck the both of you," he snaps, getting to his feet, the red panties in hand. He shoots me a glare as he twirls the chair back into place in front of my desk. "Do me a favor and actually try on Kinsey's case, huh? It's my ass on the line if you screw it up."

"What the hell's that supposed to mean?" I demand, but he's already gone, storming out of the precinct like his balls are on fire.

Just as well. I don't give a shit about his precious reputation, either. In fact, he can shove his friggin' hand-me-downs up his ass.

I can make my way up the Metro food chain on my own, fuck you very much.

Kinsey

MY PURSE AND laptop bag in one hand and a week's worth of

mail tucked beneath the other, I struggle to get the key into my apartment door when it suddenly swings open.

"Dad! What the hell?" I stumble backwards, just about snapping an ankle in these god-forsaken wedges, until he whips out a bulky arm and catches my fall.

"Is that any way to greet me?" he barks. "You think you'd be a little nicer since we haven't talked in almost two weeks."

"I've been busy." And avoiding his invitation. "How did you even get in?" I push around him and head for the kitchen. Pretty sure I never gave him a key, but that doesn't mean he didn't procure one on his own anyway.

"The manager. I told him I hadn't heard from you in days. Wanted to be sure you were safe."

I roll my eyes. "Daddy, I'm twenty-six years old. You can stop throwing your badge around to check up on me any day now."

"What if you were hurt? Or worse—lying on the bathroom floor dead?" he challenges, as I set my things on the table and spin back to him, hands on my hips. I almost collide with his chest, given my place is so dinky and he's such a big, overbearing beast.

"What if I was holed up in here with some hippie dude, smoking weed, doing shrooms, and having free-spirited, unprotected sex?"

He snorts. Actually snorts. "I don't have to worry about that with you, Kins. Never have."

Oh, really? "You never know."

He leans against the counter and crosses one ankle over the other, the fabric on the thighs of his black chinos crinkling. "You're not a wild child, princess. You might want to be, but I'm afraid you don't have it in you. Never have." He's grinning now and I want to wipe it right off his face. He's always had this goody-two shoes image of me and it's unnerving as hell.

Particularly because of super straight-laced guys he likes to throw at me. Guys like Will Vaccaro and . . . well, Ben. Don't get me wrong—I've never done a drug stronger than ibuprofen in my life—but that doesn't mean I'm vanilla to the core. Because I'm not. Not even a little.

But my father doesn't need to know that. Ever.

"Now that you can see I'm perfectly fine, is there something else you wanted?" I cringe as soon as the words are out of my mouth. So does he. God, I'm such an awful daughter sometimes. "I'm sorry, Daddy. It's just been one of those weeks."

"Everything all right at work?"

No. "Of course."

He narrows his eyes for a beat, then he quickly clenches them shut while muttering a four-letter word under his breath. "Your mother's birthday is this week, isn't it?" He gives his head a regretful shake. "I'm so sorry, Kins. I can't believe I forgot."

"It's okay." Not only was I not concerned about him forgetting, I don't expect him to make a big deal of the day anymore. He's moved on. He has something really special going with Shelby now.

"Is it okay?" he asks, tension in his brow. "It's only been five years."

"You know Mom wouldn't want you to dwell on the past. And she'd love Shelby, I'm sure of it."

My dad's face turns red and he can no longer make eye contact. I'm sure this probably has something to do with sex and being faithful to my mom, and I don't want to discuss my father's sex life any more than I want to discuss my own.

Thankfully, he changes the subject before I have to.

"Princess, I know the PD ball isn't your favorite event, but I'd really love for you to come."

Okay, maybe not that subject . . . especially because he's giving me that look. The one that always makes my good girl heart strings flutter.

"I don't even have anything to wear, Dad."

He smiles gently and pushes away from the counter to wrap me up in a hug. "Honey, you could wear your birthday—Oh, Christ, no. Don't do that." His back goes tight beneath my hands, and then relaxes as he kisses the top of my head. "You're a beautiful woman. You'll be stunning no matter what you wear."

Mmm-hmm. Pretty sure that phrase is on page one of the Father-Daughter Handbook. "Isn't Shelby going?"

"Yes, and I want you there, too. You've come since you were sixteen, Kins."

Ugh. I know, I know. But at some point, it'll have to stop, right? No one else's adult children keep up the tradition. Then again, Dad and I aren't just any father-daughter duo, either. We've been through a lot since Mom's passing.

"Fine," I sigh. "I'll go, but you're the only man I plan to dance with. In other words, no matchmaking."

He presses his lips together in a tight line, but nods. "Deal."

Uh huh. "What time should I be ready?"

"I need to be there early to make sure everything is set. Pick you up at six?"

"All right. I'll be ready." As I can be anyway.

He angles his head toward the door, and I follow after. "So, you're sure everything's good with work?" he asks, and I'm glad he's walking ahead of me, because a grimace pinches my face before I can catch it.

"Same old, same old." I shake off the reaction and the ensuing guilt, because I'm not technically lying, since this nonsense with Tally has been going on for months.

"Glad to hear it." He turns with a smile and another pang of shame niggles in my stomach. It's not that I don't want him to know about the missing inventory—I just want to figure out this mess myself.

And maybe I don't want to give Sergeant Hardass yet another reason to think I'm just a silly, incapable woman. I can follow the rules and the processes, damn it.

I have no idea what Trent's issue is with me, but it's obvious he has one, and running to Daddy will only give him more ammunition to make my life more miserable.

CHAPTER Four

Trent

SATURDAY NIGHTS ARE best spent sacked out on the couch with a few beers in the fridge and a game on the TV. Or better yet—making a soft, curvy woman pant in my bed. They're definitely not for wearing hot, uncomfortable suits to highfalutin hotels where the beer is fifteen bucks a fucking bottle.

That's my plan for tonight, though, because none of the digging around I did this week brought me closer to figuring out what the captain's cryptic comment about Investigations meant. Promotions should be given based on results and work ethic, not who puckers up best when the captain bends over.

But if he's serious, I want in. If that means I have to waste my Saturday night making pointless chit chat with the Metro's hierarchy, then I guess that's what I have to do.

Tossing some cash at the cabby, I climb out of the car in front of the venue with sweat already beaded across the back of my neck. Who the hell schedules shindigs like this for August anyway? Fuck.

"Trent?"

I glance over my shoulder as Vanessa, a receptionist from the PD's front office, gets out of the car behind me. She's wearing a snug red dress, cut all the way down to her belly button, and her heels scream a certain two-word phrase I know she'd love to whisper in my ear.

Too bad I don't screw chicks from work.

"Damn, Vanny, that's some dress." I take her hand and give it a chivalrous peck. We both know I'm no gentleman, but if I'm going to kiss ass tonight, I might as well do it all around.

She twists her painted lips into a smirk and tosses her straight blonde hair over her shoulder. "Thanks for noticing."

"I always notice, babe." Hooking her arm around mine, I escort her into the Hilton Resort in Lake Las Vegas. It's all shiny marble and glass, twinkling chandeliers, and soft, acoustic guitar coming from a live player in the middle of the foyer.

"Really? You never say anything," Vanessa whines, and I immediately regret the nice guy act. Her pout and puppy dog eyes are, case and point, why she and I will never hook up.

"Well, now I have." And I'll make damn sure I never do again.

Vanessa sighs as a kid dressed in black pants and a black button down steps forward with an awkward smile. "Good evening, sir. Ma'am. Thank you so much for your service. May I show you back to the ball?"

Vanessa nods eagerly and, for a second, I expect her bouncing tits to pop out of her dress. So does the pimple-faced dweeb, apparently. He can't take his beady eyes off of them.

"Hey . . ." I snap my fingers in front of his face. "Not cool, man."

His face turns red as he snaps his mouth shut and nods toward the wide hall that leads straight to the back of the hotel. At the end of the corridor, an elaborate arched doorway leads to a courtyard that's landscaped with tall green shrubbery and dozens of sparkling water features. Clear mini-lights adorn the shrubbery and more of the cool acoustic music hums through the warm, night air.

Beside me, Vanessa gasps. Internally, I groan.

What the hell am I doing here?

The only thing this gig has going for it is the kicked back music. The rest is just a bunch of high-society bullshit that I've never had any use for. Blowing smoke up someone's ass shouldn't have to be the way I go about getting what I want. My work on the streets should say everything that needs to be said.

"There's the bar." Vanessa points to the left, where a semi-circle of glossy wood and granite gleams against the twinkling lights overhead. An impressive spread of booze fills the shelves behind the feature, and that's at least some consolation. "Walk me over?"

"Sure." Then I'm parking my ass in the darkest corner and laying low until Captain makes his little speech.

"Well, I'll be damned!" Out of nowhere, Dez pops up in front of Vanessa and me with a cheesy ass grin. "Thought you weren't coming, Clark?"

"Fuck off," I mutter with my jaw clenched. He knows why I'm here, the prick.

He laughs before he turns his attention to Vanessa's navel. "You look thirsty, Van. Let me buy you a drink?"

"Sure," she purrs, quickly dropping my arm for his. The two of them disappear into the crowd, and I begin to stake out that coveted dark corner.

Only, my eyes fall on another dark vision instead.

Kinsey friggin' Malloy . . . in a sexy-as-hell black dress.

She stands in profile less than fifteen feet away, and I can't take my eyes off the full curve of her ass in that hip-hugging lace. Jesus Christ, the girl's got a hot, little body. High, stacked tits, and legs that are just as tight and toned as every other delicious inch of her. She's not one of those girls I'd worry about snapping in two when we fuck. She could take my punishment easily. The question is whether or not she'd give back as good as she got.

A grin tugs at my lips as I let the mental video of her climbing onto my lap play through my mind. She'd bite her lip like a nervous virgin, and I'd feel the heat of her pussy pressed against my cock. Maybe she'd grind a bit, testing the waters, but that's as far as she'd get because there's no way in hell the captain's princess would know how to handle a guy like me.

She's all bark and no bite, this one. Her little street-side tirades are nothing more than false bravado because she has her daddy to back her up. However, if I ever got Kinsey alone—on my turf and without the threat of my badge between us—there'd be no scathing glares or smart-mouthed comebacks.

I'd give her pretty lips something better to do, and then I'd make her watch as I come on those perky tits. A first for her, I'm sure, because women like Kinsey Malloy don't let assholes like me fuck with their precious virtue.

But then Miss Innocent turns away, revealing a teardrop of creamy, porcelain skin, spanning from her shoulder blades all the way down to the slope of her sweet ass, and I have to wonder . . .

Maybe this good girl has a devil on her shoulder, after all.

Maybe I should find out for sure.

Kinsey

IF I HAVE to laugh at one more corny cop joke, I'm going to throw up on Lieutenant Davies' polished shoes. Maybe stomp my three-inch Louboutin heel into the top of his foot. Or perhaps tell his wife that he's been drooling over my cleavage for the last hour without coming up for air.

Perv.

Why he's my father's best friend, I'll never understand. Then again, I don't bother trying to figure out most of what Daddy does these days. Like disappearing with Shelby and leaving me with this god-awful old man.

Flashing a polite smile at the lieutenant, I scan the room for whomever I can find first—Dad or a waiter with drinks. Fortunately, a handsome Latino man approaches with a full tray of champagne, as soon as I turn.

"Good evening, madam," he says with a sultry accent. His grin matches the lieutenant's, though the gesture is a thousand times less disturbing on him. He's at least within a decade of my age, probably younger, which could be interesting. And fun.

"Good evening to *you*." I accept a flute of bubbly with a smile of my own. What does it say about me that I'd rather spend the night talking to the waiter than my dad's friends?

"Beautiful night for a party," he says. "Where's your date?"

"Oh, I—" I spy a gold band on his left hand, dammit. Married and flirting? This place is just full of pigs tonight, isn't it? "He's here somewhere," I lie, barely resisting the urge to roll my eyes. When his grin wilts, I begrudgingly turn back to Lieutenant Davies, who's in the midst of an animated conversation with another officer.

But not just *any* other officer—Sergeant Hardass. Looking mighty fine in those dress blues.

He cleans up nice, I'll give him that, but I think I prefer the rough-around-the-edges version of him better. Not that I really *like* any of the man—there's just no point in denying that he's crazy attractive.

Too bad he's such a self-absorbed ass.

"Kinsey, you know Trent Clark, don't you?" The lieutenant waves a hand toward the man who's been nothing but a thorn in my side the past couple of weeks.

"Oh, yes. We've met." About three times too many, *not*

including his work on my vanishing inventory. "It's nice to see you again, Sergeant."

The jerk flashes a bright grin and I know—*just know*—that he's laughing his ass off inside. "Likewise." He dips his chin, which he's trimmed up instead of fully shaving. As a hot-blooded woman, I appreciate that effort, though it'd be a cold day in hell before I ever admit it out loud. "You look lovely tonight, by the way."

Uh huh, and later on tonight, he'll pull me over and tell me I'm dressed like a hooker. "Thank you," I reply, biting my tongue. "You haven't seen my dad around, have you?"

Trent shakes his head and, for a moment, I'm distracted by the twinkling lights reflecting in his eyes. Good Lord, it doesn't seem fair that a man with such an ego should also be gifted with such good looks. Those full lips and those high cheekbones . . .

He's my walking wet dream. Only I don't really like him. And I sure as hell would never sleep with him.

Tearing my eyes away, I lift the champagne to my mouth and sip. It's not the vodka cranberry I'd prefer, but if it'll help numb my sudden libido, I'll make it work.

"Will was just looking for you," Trent speaks up, and I damn near spit my drink all over the front of his uniform.

"Will Vaccaro?"

"Yup." He tips his head toward the bar. "Let's go find him."

For a long beat, I do nothing but blink at him. Trent and I aren't friends. We don't socialize except through my driver's side window or from across my desk. Two, I have no interest in Will. Not that he isn't a perfectly nice guy and, from what I hear, one hell of a cop, but that's just it—he's a cop. Like my father. Close the case, burn the file, I will *never* date a man with a badge. If I wanted to be with someone who's already committed his life to something other than me, I would've ignored the waiter's wedding ring.

"I could really use a beer." Trent lifts one dark eyebrow, and I realize he's still waiting for my response. The fact that Lieutenant Davies is staring at my boobs again makes the decision easy.

"Only if you buy me a real drink," I say, and a slow grin stretches across the Sergeant's perfectly chiseled jaw.

"Deal."

Trent

ESCORTING THE CAPTAIN'S daughter through a crowd of his closest friends works against the low profile I wanted to keep tonight, but it was either take one for the team or take Davies out to the parking lot for an old fashioned ass whooping.

The dude's old enough to be Kinsey's father, yet he was damn near foaming at the mouth, gawking at her. What's worse, I saw the dick adjustment he made when she turned away for champagne.

Now, I'm no angel. I like her dress and the way she smells a fuck lot more than I should. I won't deny that I've been semi-hard myself since she flashed all that skin either. But I'm not married with three grown children, nor am I the kind of guy to disrespect a woman by building a spank file without making my intentions known.

"You really do look nice tonight," I tell her as we weave through the sea of blue uniforms and shimmering gowns. "The back of that dress . . ." I let out a low whistle and Kinsey shoots me a sidelong glance.

"Seriously, Trent?"

"I'm just saying what every man here is thinking right now, Kins—you're fucking hot."

She slows her pace and, because we're arm in arm, so do I. "I'm not sure if I should be flattered or offended."

"It's a compliment, not an insult."

"Coming from you that's hard to believe."

I lift a shoulder and give her a crooked grin. "You only know the man behind the badge, princess."

"Don't call me that," she snaps, but her bark is more like a nibble. An uncertain curiosity that confirms my initial suspicion—Kinsey might sell kinky lingerie and dress like a sex kitten, but she's more apt to cuddle than leave scratches down a man's back.

"You're sexy when you're annoyed. Anyone ever tell you that?" Might as well have fun and push her buttons a little harder. Reaching up, I smooth a lock of her hair between my fingers. She's got the messy up-do thing going on and the dark, silky tendrils that fall around her face are gorgeous as hell. All too easily, I can imagine how her pretty hair would look, fanned out across my pillow as I push her back on my bed and feast between her legs. I'd make her kitty purr like it's never before, and I'd enjoy every friggin' second of it.

"Don't touch me, either," she says, though her tone is weak and her cheeks are flushed. Her eyes are also glued to my mouth, like she knows exactly what I'm thinking.

"Just admiring, Kins. No harm in that, is there?"

Her lips part slightly and the tip of her tongue peeks out just enough to make my balls ache. "I don't trust you, Sergeant."

I wouldn't trust me either if I were her. "Ah, but you hardly know me, remember?"

"You're trouble with a capital T. That's all I need to know."

CHAPTER Five

Kinsey

NEVER BEFORE HAS trouble been so tempting.

Trent Clark is the kind of man that could ruin me in one night, and not with wine and roses. No, he'd leave me with body aches and residual tremors, torn panties and bruised lips. I can see the promise in his eyes as clearly as I can see that perfect shade of blue. He'd give me everything Ben couldn't and then he'd walk away with a smile.

I shouldn't want him.

He's a cop who works for my father. He's been nothing but a pain in my ass for weeks, and now he's working my theft case.

But he looks at me tonight like he wants to eat me alive and, damn it, if I don't want him to do just that.

It's been a while since I've played for the sake of playing. I promised myself that once I turned twenty-six—and formally climbed the hill to thirty—I'd stop looking for guys who could only indulge that one part of me. Ben was my first attempt at making good on that promise, but look how that turned out. Sex may not be everything, but it's definitely something.

Something I haven't had in months.

Leaning close with his rough fingertips dancing along my bare arm, Trent rasps in my ear, "Who's looking at who now, princess?"

"Just paying back the favor."

"Yeah? You like what you see?"

Way more than I should.

"How about we get that drink?" I paste on a smile and do my damnedest to ignore the tension pulsing between us. Nothing good could come of getting messed up with a guy like Trent, even if my greedy libido says otherwise.

Chuckling softly, he takes his time stepping back. "Should've called it."

"Excuse me?"

"Nothing." He knuckles his nose and lifts his chin toward the bar. "Looks like Will found your old man."

"Oh." I toe up and sure enough, Dad's clapping Will on the back while Shelby grins between the two of them.

God help me.

Chuckling, Trent urges me forward until Dad spots us.

"Princess!" His eyes light up and he waves me to his side anxiously. "Will and I were just talking about you."

Of course they were. "All good, I hope."

"Absolutely. I told him how excited you are to help out with the children's back-to-school program this year."

Um, what?

"You're very generous to volunteer your time, Kinsey." Will's smile is as tight as my own, and I have no doubt that he knows my father is full of shit.

"Well, well," Dad says suddenly, glancing at his watch. "It's just about time for announcements and recognition. Detective, could you keep an eye on my daughter while I take care of business?"

Will clears his throat uncomfortably, but nods nonetheless. "Yes, sir."

Really? I'm twenty-six, not a kindergartener.

"See you soon, princess." Dad presses a kiss to my temple and then he's off, escorting Shelby toward the stage.

As soon as they're out of earshot, I turn to Will. "You know I don't need a babysitter, right?"

He chuckles. "Not sure, Kins. You *did* walk over here with Trent."

Beside him, Sergeant Hardass snorts. "Fuck you, too, man."

"Just calling it like I see it." Will lifts both hands in the air. "Keeping company with you would make me question anyone's judgment."

I roll my eyes and glance at the bar with envy. Trent notices.

"I still owe you that drink," he says, stepping forward with his hands tucked in his pockets.

"Right now, I could use five."

He tips his head toward Will. "If my old man wanted me to hook up with this asshole, I'd drink myself to death, too."

Will makes a disgruntled sound, but the color in his face gives him away. He hates this crap with my dad as much as I do.

"Go on," I tell my father's dream son-in-law. "I'm fine. And I promise I'll make him stop this nonsense once and for all."

His jaw pulses as his gaze shifts between Trent and me. "Don't get her drunk," he warns his friend.

"She's a big girl, Vaccaro. I'm not going to babysit her anymore than you would have."

"Hello!" I wave a hand in the air. "I'm right here!"

Will's eyes narrow in on Trent, blatantly ignoring me. "She's a case. Don't forget that."

"Oh, so I need a caregiver now, too?" Trent scoffs, before he looks back to me. "Come on, Kins. Let's go finds the crayons and finger paints."

Five minutes later, I'm sipping vodka cranberry and he's downing a bottle of Guinness.

"Thanks for saving me from Lieutenant Davies, by the way. I'm assuming that's why you pretended Will was looking for me?"

"Nah, I just wanted to harass you." He winks and I roll my eyes, as my dad and a mass of higher-ranking officers crowd around the front of the podium while the Sheriff takes to the stage. They look like a bunch of eager puppies, waiting for their treat, and I suppose, in a way, they are.

"What's with the harassment anyway? Am I that easy of a target?"

"Kind of. And like I said before . . ." He flashes a grin. "You're fucking hot."

I should smack him, but instead I smile. "I think I like you better without the badge."

"Eh, don't give me too much credit. I'm still a fucker, trust me."

Biting back a bark of laughter, I turn my attention to the stage and, together, Trent and I stand in silence while the Sheriff gives his annual speech. His words are full of pride and praise for each of the men and women who serve as Metro PD officers and, despite my distaste for so many things *cop*, I couldn't agree more. I'm proud of the work my dad does, even if his job has made it difficult for him to just be *Dad* and not *nosey cop Dad*.

From the corner of my eye, I see Trent's shoulders pull back a little further with every accolade. In the distance, my dad's stature is the same. Stoic. Proud. Confident. All well deserved, as far as I'm concerned, though if Sergeant Hardass wanted to cut me some slack, I wouldn't complain.

Several of the directors and captains follow the Sheriff, each speaking on behalf of their units. A few of them announce officer retirements and transfers, and I can't help but notice the tension setting into Trent's posture. His jaw is clenched and the tendons in his neck strain. I'm not sure he's even breathing, to be honest, and I have to wonder what's brought on the quiet, albeit palpable, reaction.

Finally, my dad takes the stage and I'm torn between listening to his words and making sure Sergeant Hardass doesn't stroke out next to me.

"Good evening, comrades, family, and friends," Daddy begins, slowly scanning the crowd until his gaze finally lands on me, and he smiles. I return the gesture complete with a subtly blown kiss, before he continues on again. He shares stories from the past year in a light, jovial voice, until suddenly his tone changes. "I've spent the past twenty-five years with the Metro PD," he says. "I worked my way up from Strip patrol to homicide investigations and then I came back to Tourism Safety as a captain ten years ago. I've loved every moment of my time here, but some were more enjoyable than others."

Why the hell does this speech suddenly sound like goodbye?

"It's with great pride—and a little sadness," he continues on, "that I share with you tonight my intentions to leave Tourism for a new role as Captain of the Homicide and Sex Crimes Unit. Maybe I'm wired wrong, but my heart belongs to homicide and I'm excited as hell to go back."

"What?" My mouth falls open as the crowd erupts with applause. He never said a word about making a change. Never even hinted that he wanted to go back to the blood and gore. "I can't believe this."

"No shit," Trent mutters beside me. "Sneaky bastard."

"You didn't know either?"

He lifts his beer and shakes his head. "Nope. Not a clue. In fact—" Trent stops short when my father's voice rings through the sound system again.

"Shelby, dear, could you please join me on stage?"

Oh for Pete's sake, now what?

The sergeant and I watch in stunned silence as Dad meets his girlfriend at the top of the stairs and then leads her to the center of the stage.

"Tonight's a big night for me, darlin'," he says into the hand-held mic. "And I'm wondering if you'd make it even more special."

When my father hits his knee in front of Shelby, my gasp is loud enough for everyone to hear.

When he takes the tiny box from the pocket of his dress blues, the room begins to spin.

When he pops the question—and she says yes—I turn and run.

Trent

I CATCH UP to Kinsey outside the front foyer where she stops to yank off her shoes.

"Leave me alone, Trent. I'm not in the mood for your shit right now." Breathless, she points a glittery heel at me and I see the tears welling up in her dark eyes.

"Can't do that, Kins. You're upset." My own aggravation aside, letting her run off into the night goes against my better judgment. I may be off duty, but protecting others has been hardwired in my moral fiber.

"I'm not a freaking child!" she hollers, and behind her, one of the entrance security guards dips his chin toward the radio on his shoulder.

"Come on. Let's get you out of here. Somewhere you can cool off." *Before you cause a scene.* I reach for her arm, but she snatches it away and marches barefoot to the curb. A few yards away, a waiting cab shifts into gear and approaches.

"I'm going home," she snaps. "And the last damn thing I plan to do is *cool off*."

God, she's cute when she's pissed. I open the car door for her and she climbs inside with a huff. I drop in after her and tell the cabby to head toward Henderson. I expect her to argue about me tagging along, but she's too caught up in her anger.

"How could he do this?" She pushes her hands into her hair. "I mean, I love Shelby. I'm happy for them, but a little notice would have been nice, you know? And he's going back to Homicide? What is that about?"

"You got me, Kins." She sure as hell isn't the only one who's surprised.

"And what was up with the Iron Man act back there? I was worried you were going to pass out on me!"

I lift a shoulder and gaze out the window as the cabby merges onto the interstate. "Just thinking about how I should've stayed home tonight, that's all."

"Yeah, no kidding." Kinsey crosses her arms over her chest and, for the next fifteen minutes, we both pretend to enjoy the church music on the cabby's radio.

Finally, Kinsey clears her throat. "We're almost to my place. If you could just drop me off at the restaurant on the next block, that'd be great."

"Sure thing," the cab driver says, and I pinch the bridge of my nose.

Kinsey doesn't live in this neighborhood. Close, but not close enough. I don't say anything, though, as the car slows in front of an Italian place. It's early enough in the evening that the place is still serving food, so it's possible she's just hungry.

But my gut says she's trying to bail.

She begins to dig in her purse for the fare, but I put a hand on her arm. "The ride's on me tonight, princess."

For a moment, she blinks up at me with those pretty brown

eyes. Even with frustration burning in their depths, they're intoxicating. I wish tonight could've ended differently, so maybe I could've spent a little more time enjoying them.

"Thank you." Her gaze drops to my chest as she sucks in a breath. "I'm sorry for being such a bitch tonight. I took my anger out on you and I—"

Pressing a finger lightly to her lips, I hush her. "Already forgotten, Kins."

She slowly meets my eyes again, swallowing hard. "Maybe there's more to the guy behind the badge than I thought."

Probably, but I'm still at least eighty-percent prick. The proof being that I can't stop thinking about her on her knees.

Flashing another grateful smile, she gets out of the car and hurries down the street toward the restaurant's entrance.

"Where to next, sir?" the cab driver asks, as I dig a fifty from my wallet.

"Actually, this is my stop, too." I pass the cash over the seat and he nods. "Keep the change and have a good night."

Climbing out into the balmy night, I scan the street for Kinsey, but she's nowhere to be seen.

Ducking into the darkened doorway of a closed bookstore, I wait, giving her two minutes to show back up again, thinking she's lost me.

Sure as shit, the telltale click of heels on the sidewalk sounds only moments later. She passes by the darkened doorway, headed toward the seedier side of the neighborhood.

I watch her until she hits the end of the block and turns right, then I hurry behind, careful not to be seen or heard. Hitting the end of the sidewalk, I catch a glimpse of her just as she enters a bar.

But not just any bar—a dive bar. Franco's, to be exact. The best place in the neighborhood to grab a cold draft beer or score a random hook up. The odds are about the same, especially on a Saturday night.

How do I know?

This is my neighborhood and this is my bar.

CHAPTER
Six

Kinsey

I HAVEN'T HIT up Franco's in years. Since my freshman year of college actually, when I wasn't even legal to drink. Daddy's little girl was something of a rebel back then, trying to get away with anything and everything I hadn't been able to under Hitler's roof. It helped that Franco's bouncer had been a friend from school and the bartender had been too busy to check IDs.

I remember that night at Franco's for one reason and one reason only—I lost my virginity that night. In the men's bathroom. To a guy named Mohawk, who was at least twenty-five to my eighteen. He wasn't the kind of guy I could ever bring home to Mom and Dad, with his jet black mohawk (shockingly) and five facial piercings. He was in a band, and he gave me so much more than he took that night.

Sliding onto the only vacant stool at the far end of the bar, I smile to myself. I'm not a sexual deviant by any means. I'm not into the really weird shit . . . or at least not yet. But I do appreciate a pair of rough hands and a dirty, vulgar mouth more than most. And maybe it's ridiculous, but after months of taking care of business by myself, paired with my pissy mood, I need another version of Mohawk tonight.

Franco's brought me luck once, so maybe I'll get lucky and lightning will strike twice.

"What can I get for you, gorgeous?" the handsome bartender asks, as he leans across the bar, showing off some wickedly muscled forearms, complete with tats.

"I'll start with a shot of Gentleman, and follow up with a tall Whiskey Sling."

He arches an eyebrow at my matter-of-fact order and something about that expression rings familiar. "You here alone?" he asks, and damn if he doesn't sound just like Hardass and Will.

What-the-hell-ever.

"For now," I lie. "I'm meeting a friend."

Lifting his chin, he goes to work on my shot. While I down that and relish in the burn, he mixes the whiskey and lemon concoction.

"That's an awfully pretty dress for this part of town and that kind of drink. What time will your friend be here?"

"When he gets here," I say with a smile. Truth is, he may already be here. If Hunky Forearms would leave me alone, I could get a better look around.

"Don't get yourself into trouble before then," he warns before going back to work further down the bar.

Thank God. Crossing my legs, I spin on the stool so I can see the pool tables and dart boards. My focus falls almost immediately on a tall, athletic looking guy in a pair of jeans and black T-shirt. Inconspicuous enough, except for the tattoo creeping up the side of his neck and the short, dirty blond ponytail tied at the back of his head. He has a Charlie Hunnam vibe going on, and I'm hopeful.

I watch him for a few more minutes, until he glances over, sees me and smiles. I give a subtle wave and he trades his pool stick for a mug of beer before coming over.

"You're a shark out there," I say above the Aerosmith humming through the sound system. "I'm impressed."

He laughs and the sound is rich and deep, just like I like.

"Easy to look good when the competition sucks."

Yes, I noticed, but I figured I'd stroke his ego anyway. "I'm Kinsey," I say, offering my hand.

"Chase."

"Nice to meet you, Chase." I clink my drink against his mug and he leans in as the music seems to get louder.

"I've never seen you here before. Are you new to the area?"

"Nope. Born and raised in LV. Just passing through on my way home tonight."

"Ah. So you're by yourself?" I nod and a crooked grin slides across his face. "Why don't you come over and hang with me and my friends? I'll grab your next drink."

I take him up on the offer and, twenty minutes later, I'm in the midst of a game, partnered with my new friend.

"Right there," he says, pointing to an open shot that I could easily sink. Instead, I play nervous. "You want some help?"

"Could you?"

Chase grins and all too eagerly sidles up behind me as I line up the shot. His hips press against my ass as he leans down, over my back. He's big and overwhelming, and he'd toss me around like a rag doll, I just know he would. My blood rolls a little hotter just thinking about how easily I could let him own me, and that's both exciting and terrifying at the same time.

I've been with six guys in the past eight years. I'm not a slut, but I do have slutty tendencies and, right now, they crave indulgence. The promise I made myself says I shouldn't take this any further, but the pulse beating between my legs says why the hell not?

With Chase's hand wrapped around mine, I shoot . . . and not only sink my solid, but the eight ball, too. *Shit.*

His friends whoop and holler about their win, and my confidence sinks to my toes.

What am I doing? Do I honestly want to hook up with a

random guy just because I have an itch? Just because the night didn't go my way?

"Can you excuse me for a minute?" I ask Chase, who dips his chin without hesitation.

Grabbing my purse, I hurry to the hall at the back of the bar, quickly finding the women's bathroom at the very end of the narrow corridor.

Inside, I stare at myself in the mirror, trying to catch my suddenly frantic breath. I should've gone home. Hell, I should've never *left* home. Then I never would've ended up in this battle of moral will.

The bathroom door creaks open behind me and, in the reflection, a man in a tight white T-shirt and dark washed jeans steps in, flipping the lock behind him. I gasp as he takes two big steps forward and slides a callused hand around my mouth.

"Don't even think about it," he rasps in my ear, with the heat and muscle of his upper body pressing firmly against the bare skin on my back. He's bigger than Chase, and there's a dangerous glint in his crystal blue eyes as he watches me in the mirror. "You shouldn't be here, princess. Bad things can happen to pretty girls like you in this part of town."

I try to answer, but he only grips me harder, pinning my pelvis to the counter with his hips.

"What's your game, Kinsey, huh?" His breath is hot against the side of my neck as he trails his nose and parted lips to the soft spot behind my ear. "You come here looking for trouble?"

My first instinct is to shake my head, but I'm not sure there's any sense in lying.

"That's it, isn't it?" He smiles against my ear before nipping roughly at my lobe and abrading my skin with his harsh stubble. A shudder of desire races down my spine as I realize he's hard against my ass. "I've got no problem with you doing what you've gotta do, princess, but when you step into my bar, you play by my rules. You get me?"

I nod, but I have no idea what he's talking about. His bar? And where the hell did he get these clothes from?

"Good girl." The hand on my mouth loosens slightly, but the one curled around my hip digs deep. "So here's how it's going to go, Kins. You get two choices. One, you get your sweet ass into my truck and I take you home right now."

I'll pass. Unless he plans on coming inside.

"Or two, you forget the fuckwad at the pool table and you come upstairs with me. No questions, no expectations, definitely no promises . . ."

That. I want that.

Trent grins at me in the mirror and drops his hand. "You're a dirty little girl, aren't you, princess?"

Cheeks flushed and nostrils flaring, I lick my lips. "I guess you'll see."

His eyes narrow slightly, but his smirk stretches wide. "So we're going with the second option?"

I shake my head. "I'm not going upstairs with you."

He quirks an eyebrow as I push back against his dick.

"I want you to fuck me right here."

Trent

BLOOD SURGES THROUGH my cock when those sweet words roll off her tongue. I know fucking around with her is going to come back to bite me in the ass, but right now it seems like a small price to pay.

Winding my fingers in her hair, I tug her head back, exposing that long line of soft, creamy skin running all the way down to her collarbone. I could kiss her pretty skin. Maybe tease a little. But the fire in her eyes says she's craving something more.

So I lick . . . and then I bite, only momentarily soothing away the sting with my tongue. With each new assault, her curvy little ass writhes back against my swollen dick, greedily begging for punishment.

"And here I thought you were one of the quiet ones," I taunt her before I suck hard on her collarbone, drawing the sexiest little moan from her lips and probably leaving a mark, too. "But you're not really quiet at all, are you?"

She shakes her head and reaches around between us, anxiously trying to palm my shaft. "Are you going to fuck me or not?"

"So damn impatient," I chuckle, as my fingers slide down her hips and then roughly tug up the tight lace of her dress. The fleshy swell of her perfect ass pops free and I groan.

No panties.

"You ditch the thong, Kins, or were you bare like this when you stood beside me at the ball?"

"Didn't go with the dress," she pants, her hand wrapped around what it can of my cock, squeezing. "Come on, Sergeant. Either show me what you've got, or let me go so I can do the work."

Fucking hell. How could I have been so wrong about this girl?

"Your daddy forget to teach you manners, princess?"

She opens her mouth to respond, but the crack of my hand across her ass turns her response into a gasp . . . and then a wicked little smile.

"I already told you that, in my bar, I'm in charge. You forget that already?"

Something absolutely fucking beautiful falls over her face as she bites her lip and shakes her head. "I'm sorry."

"Damn right, you are." Jerking her around, I push her to her knees. "How about you apologize properly?"

Eye level with my fly, she licks her lips and bats those gorgeous eyes. For a moment, I think she's going to change her mind, but then her adept little fingers make quick work of loosening my belt.

I wind my hands in her hair as she unsnaps and lowers my fly, inch by painful inch, until my cock springs free in her face.

"Jesus . . ." Her lips part and her cheeks flush, and I'm pretty damn sure those are stars in her eyes. "All of this for me?"

"All yours, baby. All night, too. Especially when you bent over that pool table out there." I brush a strand of hair behind her ear as she wraps a hand around my dick and strokes. "Do you do this often, Kins? Let strange men fuck you in dive bar bathrooms?"

She shakes her head and an odd sense of relief blooms in my gut. Nothing's going to stop me from giving her exactly what she wants tonight, but I'd rather not be a contribution to a bigger problem.

"Ah, yeah . . ." I groan when her hot, wet mouth opens wide and takes my cock. Stretched into the perfect O, her painted lips slide down my shaft until I hit the back of her throat. Tears spring into those dark eyes, but she doesn't stop.

Back and forth she works me, one hand curled around the root, while her tongue rubs and swirls around my head. Over and over again, she bobs deep, swallowing me down like a fucking porn star.

"Dirty, dirty princess . . ." I wipe away a tear with the pad of my thumb. "I think she likes choking on my cock."

Her eyes flutter shut as she hums, and the vibration is friggin' heaven. My abs twitch and pressure builds tight at the base of my spine. I could blow down her throat in a heartbeat, but this is still her game, my rules or not. I let her go for a bit, sucking my cock like it's her last meal, until I can't take it anymore.

"Get up." I grasp her arm and pull her to her feet, my mouth crashing down on hers as I lift her to the counter. Her lips are soft and her tongue is sweet, but she kisses with a hunger so fierce it makes my head spin.

Kinsey's not a whore—she's just a woman who's been denied a proper fucking.

Lucky for her, I know how to use my dick.

"You ready to sing, baby?" I ask, digging out the condom I stashed less than a half hour ago.

She leans back on her palms, spreads her knees wide, and shows off every bit of that pretty pink pussy. There's a dangerously sexy gleam in those dark eyes as she watches me roll on the rubber. Her tits, still wrapped tight in her dress, heave with every anxious breath she takes.

She's a goddamn vision. A desperate, needy temptation that I couldn't have denied, even if I'd wanted to, and I have to wonder . . .

Who's *really* getting fucked here?

CHAPTER
Seven

Kinsey

TRENT PUSHES DOWN his jeans and, with an arm around my waist, tugs me to the edge of the counter. The tiny bathroom already smells like sex and I realize it's all me. He's had me primed and ready to go for hours and, if I'm honest, he's the real reason I'm here tonight. The irony of this place being his—or whatever he meant by that—is damn interesting.

I reach for his cock and try to align him with my pussy, but he slaps away my hand and, damn, if I don't love that sting.

"Whose rules, Kins?"

"Yours," I pant. God, I need him inside. I want to feel that delicious burn of being taken and stretched. That hard friction of body on body. The sweet, overwhelming sensation of being completely freaking owned.

"You're so goddamn pretty when you're desperate," he says, dropping his forehead down against mine while he grasps his cock and rubs the thick head over my aching clit.

A shudder slides down my spine and my pussy clenches in anticipation. A crooked grin lifts one side of his mouth as he repeats the motion again and again, until I cry out from the agony of it.

"Fuck!" I shake so hard that my fingertips dig into the cool countertop to keep myself upright. I want to come so badly, but his touch is just a little too gentle. Close, but not close enough.

"What do you need, baby? Tell me."

"Harder," I beg, my voice hoarse. Edgy. Raw.

"Like this?" He replaces his cock with the rough pad of his thumb, giving my clit the concentrated friction it craves.

"Oh, *Godddd* . . ." My low moan melds into a greedy cry as the pressure winds tight, pulsing right there on the edge of release.

"Come on, princess. I know you want to come. You wouldn't be here tonight if you didn't." He slides two fingers inside and begins pumping slowly, using the heel of his palm to rub my swollen clit while he loosens me up to three fingers.

His cock is hot and long resting on my thigh, and it would be so easy to guide him inside and take what I want.

"Yeah, baby, I could fuck this orgasm out of you, but you've gone through all this trouble. The least I can do is give you more than one."

Oh, fuck, yes. Please.

Suddenly, his other hand connects with the side of my ass and I jump. The motion jars the heel of his hand against my clit and his fingers grip inside of me *just . . . right*.

"Yes, yes, yes . . ." I reach between my legs and grip his hand, holding him in place, with his hand cupped like a fist, half in my pussy and half out, absolutely tormenting me.

All that tight tension inside and all that incredible friction outside, hard and rough . . .

My hips lift off the counter, fucking his hand for all it's worth, until I shatter. Absolutely fucking shatter into a million irreparable pieces.

"Trent!" I don't hold back my cry and he doesn't hold back, either, when he slams his cock inside my still-fluttering pussy.

"Ah, princess, you feel so fucking good." Forehead against mine again, he steals a breathless kiss. "Better than I imagined."

He's thought about this? God.

Slowly, he begins to fuck me, face-to-face, long and deep. Our mingled breathing is frantic and hot, and in seconds I come again, the orgasm ripping through me like an earthquake.

He grunts his approval and wraps an arm around my back, holding me in place as his thrusts grow harder and harder. He's so deep inside, sliding along nerves and pleasure points I haven't felt in a long time.

I slide one hand into his hair, taking his mouth again in a heady kiss, while the other finds his ass, flexing tight as he pistons in and out of me like a machine.

Definitely a hard ass. Definitely going to ruin me, too.

"Goddamn, Kins . . ." His nostrils flare and blue-hot flames blaze in his eyes, as perspiration beads across his forehead. "All night long you stood next to me bare. All night long I could've fucking had this . . ."

"All yours," I tell him. "Any time you want it."

Something flashes in his eyes, and then he reaches between us and pinches my clit. I bite my lip to keep from screaming, but I can't hold back the low, rumbling groan in my chest.

He's going to blow my mind for a third time and that hasn't happened . . . ever.

"Do it, princess." His hand winds in my hair, tugging hard so that my eyes are lined up with his. So I can't question his meaning. "I want to feel your tight little cunt grip me again. I want you to come so hard the whole fucking bar knows how good I gave it to you."

Yes! My God, how does he know? How does he—

He hikes me off the counter and slams my back into the wall with nothing but his hand and arm as cushion.

"Shit, Trent! *Fuckkkk!*" I lose it all over again, coming so hard my ears ring. He follows after, grunting hard as he unloads inside of me.

Both of us breathing hard, he presses his forehead to mine and kisses me gently. A complete one-eighty from possessive kisses only moments ago. "Feel better?"

Oh, he has no idea. "Much," I pant. "That was amazing."

He smiles against my lips. "Wouldn't have been half as good with that other loser."

God. Closing my eyes, I take a moment to catch my breath. "Where the hell did you come from anyway? In different clothes."

"Bought the bar with my brothers a couple of years ago," he says, as he discards the condom in the trash. "I'm staying upstairs while my townhouse is being renovated."

So that's why the bartender looked familiar. "How many brothers?"

"Two. You met Trav at the bar."

"Ah." I shimmy my dress back into place, the slow realization of what we've just done settling in. "I just nailed a cop."

"In a bar," he adds, winking at me in the mirror as he washes his hands. "Is this your thing or . . . ?"

"God, no." I shake my head adamantly. "I mean, maybe a little, but it's been more fantasy than reality." Except for that one time.

He grabs some paper towels and turns back to me, his jeans still undone at his waist. His hair is a mess from my hands and his T-shirt somehow has my lipstick on the collar. "Why Franco's?" he asks. "Don't tell me it's a coincidence that you ended up here, because I watched you. You knew where you were going."

He's right. Ending up in the neighborhood was pure luck, but as soon as my heels hit the pavement outside of the cab, I knew where I'd end up. I only hoped it'd work out like this. That it happened with Trent is probably both a blessing and a curse. Only time will tell which.

"I was here once a long time ago," I admit.

"And what," he laughs, " . . . it was such a memorable experience, you had to come back? Shit, Kins, this place doesn't look any better now than it did ten years ago. You sure as fuck don't belong here during the daylight, let alone at night in a dress like that."

"Oh, but it's okay for you?" I snap, my chin pulled in.

"I pay the mortgage every month and I also carry a badge in my back pocket, so yeah, babe, it is okay for me." He tosses the paper towel, zips up, and stalks forward, his big hands smoothing back over my hips. "That's okay, Kins. You don't have to tell me what really brought you here," he says softly. "We all have our secrets, now don't we?"

My face flames hot, which is absolutely ridiculous. I just shamelessly begged him to fuck me and now I'm blushing like a preteen. "Keep this one between us?"

He gives his head a decisive nod. "I fucked the captain's daughter, princess. Not something I'm going to write in the sky."

A small smile tickles at the corner of my mouth. "Do you think you could stop pulling me over now?"

His smoldering, sated eyes widen. "Not a chance, babe."

Trent

I PULL INTO Kinsey's driveway on the other side of Henderson just after ten o'clock. She yawns from the passenger seat of my truck, but I still kill the engine. Whatever meaningless shit just happened between us at the bar, Kinsey is not the kind of girl I can just drop off at the curb and go on my merry way. She might think she is—or she might want to be—but there's a whole other side to her that needs something more.

I'm not the guy to give it to her, but I like her enough not to be an ass. For now, I'll give her what she probably doesn't even know she needs. When her case is over, I'll walk away.

"Thank you for the ride," she says softly, unbuckling her seatbelt. "I still stand by the fact that I could have grabbed a cab."

"But would you have come home?" I wink, and she shoves at my shoulder.

"Hey now. I might like a dirty romp from time to time, but I wouldn't go looking for guy number two still smelling like guy number one."

But isn't that an interesting thought? "Have you ever done that?"

She glances over at me with a frown. "I just said I wouldn't."

"I mean two guys. At once."

Her cheeks darken in the dash light glow. "No. Not that I haven't been curious."

Wow. It really is the quiet ones, isn't it?

"Don't." She shakes her head, though she laughs as she does it. "Don't look at me like you think I'm crazy, because I can guarantee you've done it. Probably more than once."

"Two dudes?" I chuckle. "Nah, not really my thing, princess."

She tries to swat at me again, but I catch her wrist and pull her hand to my mouth, kissing her knuckles. Then I reach down and hit the button, moving my seat all the way back.

"Come on," I say, patting my lap.

"What?" Her eyes go wide and her lips part.

"Climb on board, princess. Before the train leaves the station."

"I'm not fucking you in my driveway, Trent." She rolls her eyes, but I can see her scanning the lot of her apartment complex. She lives in a quiet neighborhood. Mostly older couples. No kids. No teenagers coming and going at this time of the night who might accidentally see something they shouldn't.

"Not asking you to fuck me in your driveway, Kins. Now get your sweet ass over here."

She shakes her head, but when I give her hand a tug, she tosses her purse onto the dash and sighs. "Fine, but only because you smell good."

I chuckle as she takes off her shoes and climbs over the console, a knee on each side of my thighs. It's not the most comfortable position in the world, but with her legs spread, her dress creeps up toward her waist, giving me another glorified view of her sweet spot.

I should be a gentleman and walk her to her door, but I slide my fingers over her cleft instead, loving her quick intake of breath when my fingertips brush her clit.

"What part of being with two guys turns you on the most?" I ask, playing her gently. She's still swollen from the bathroom and I want this to be as good for her now as it was the first time.

Pressing her hands against my chest, she closes her eyes and for the longest moment, just lets me touch her. The look on her face is so fucking calm. The polar opposite of the fiery hunger that had been there just a short time ago.

"Four hands," she sighs. "Two mouths, two dicks . . . all that pleasure at once."

Her eyes are still closed, so I watch her . . . and wonder if she knows how breathtaking she is like this. Completely open, not just physically but emotionally, too. The Kinsey I've known for the past couple of years has always been so closed off. So tense. So untouchable. Until now.

Unable to stop myself, I reach up and pluck out one of the pins barely holding her hair in place. The urge to break her down as much as she'll let me is strong. So fucking strong that it rattles me a bit. I don't do personal shit for other people unless I'm on the clock. I do me and only me.

But tonight I want to do her.

"What are you doing?" she whispers, but I hush her by sliding a finger inside. "God," she breathes. "That feels so good."

"Just enjoy it," I whisper back, removing another pin and then five, until her hair falls over her shoulders, in thick, dark waves.

"So fucking pretty," I murmur, letting my fingers thread through the silk while the others slip in and out of her wet, welcoming body.

Her eyes flutter open and her chest begins to rise and fall a little faster with every breath she takes. "My God, what are you doing to me?" she pants, her hips slowly working against my hand.

"Hands everywhere, princess. Isn't that your fantasy?" And fuck if it isn't quickly becoming mine.

Her gaze locks on mine as she lifts and circles her ass, taking what she wants down below, while I take what I want up top. I know how chicks feel about having their hair played with, but what she doesn't know is that I like it, too.

Doing her tonight, my ass.

I've wanted to fuck up Kinsey's perfect existence since I laid eyes on her, three years ago. Why? Because she's the kind of woman that can screw with a guy's head. Make him start thinking about shit he has no business thinking about. Especially not a guy like me.

"Why do you care what I want?" she whispers, and her eyes are so fucking pretty, all half-lidded and full of lust. "You don't even like me."

"Yeah, I do, Kins." She's sweet when she's not spitting fire at me, and both versions make me hot as hell. The thing is, I can't—and I won't—give her more than this. If she needs demanding hands and dirty words . . . Maybe a hard fuck every now and again, I'm her guy. Shit, her vulnerability does as much for me as it does her.

But that's all this will ever be. Me scratching her itch, because I can't let her take a chance on messing with someone who won't respect her limits.

I know Kinsey's secret, but she doesn't know mine.

And, if I have it my way, she never will.

CHAPTER Eight

Trent

"TELL ME YOU didn't sleep with her."

I glance up from my paperwork as Will slams both of his hands down on my desk bright and early Monday morning. His dark eyes bore into mine, trying to dig out the truth.

"Who? Kinsey?" I never tell him the truth about my personal life. Hell, I never tell anyone the truth, because honesty always comes around to bite me in the ass one way or another. "Why the hell would you think that?"

"You left with her."

"Yeah. To make sure she got home safe."

Will's jaw tightens as he continues to stare.

"What?" I throw a hand in the air. "She was upset. The captain didn't tell her about changing jobs or that he was going to propose. Ended up being one hell of a night for her."

"Uh huh." He pushes a hand through his hair and huffs out a frustrated breath. "Dude, you know you can't fuck around with clients."

"No shit, Sherlock." I know the rules, though when it came to indulging Kinsey and keeping her away from the pool prick, I had no problem throwing them out the window.

"Just because you were pissed that the captain's announcement wasn't what you thought it would be—"

"Hold up." I raise another hand and shake my head. "Don't go around accusing me of that kind of bogus bullshit." I might not be the most ethical guy when it comes to women, but I'm not so shallow that I'd bang the captain's daughter just because he fucked me over.

I fucked Kinsey because we both wanted it, plain and simple.

"Unless, of course, the real issue is that I took her home and you didn't," I say, knowing damn well what his reaction will be.

His face pinches and he pushes off my desk. "Shut the hell up, man."

"All right then. No reason to get pissed off when I ended up doing you a favor."

He makes a wry sound, and then drops down into Dez's empty chair. He's out on patrol this morning and in an hour I'll join him. Good ol' Monday morning on the Strip.

"But since you brought her up, Kinsey has a solid lead on the perp. An employee."

"Catch any of it on surveillance?"

I explain about the camera system being down and why Kinsey thinks this Tally chick is the one snatching the goods. "We're going to watch the place at closing a couple nights this weekend. See if we can catch her."

Will blinks and, again, I know what he's thinking before he even says it. "We?"

"Yeah. At this point, I don't have any reason to stop this chick and search her, unless Kinsey tells me that something's been stolen."

"You're out of your fucking mind."

"Gotta do what's going to work, no?"

"No wonder you're still on patrol."

"Fuck you." I'm bitter because I know he's probably right. So sue me—I had a moment of weakness when Kinsey proposed her idea. Obviously, the whole idea of staking out the Mile employee parking ramp is pretty Mayberry in about 1955, but the background check I did on Tally shows it's probably the best approach. She's got a couple of battery charges, so my presence should prevent anything from happening to Kinsey if this girl decides to flip out. Without camera footage from inside the store, there's not much else I can do.

Short of fixing the damn cameras myself, anyway.

"You know I put in a good word for you, right?"

My eyes snap up to my buddy, reclined in the chair, with his arms folded behind his head. "For what?"

"For Investigations. With Deputy Chief Marcos."

No shit. "Why would you do that?"

"Because you're not a bad cop when you're not thinking with your dick."

I give a bark of laughter. "Oh, really."

"I'm serious, Clark. And rumor has it there really is an opening coming up. In Theft. I know it isn't as exciting as dead pervs in thongs, but it's a foot in the door."

The back of my neck begins to burn as the thought of finally getting the hell off patrol settles in. I haven't let myself fully entertain the idea, because I hate being let down. But Will wouldn't tell me this if he didn't think there was a legitimate chance I could get in.

"What'd Marcos say?"

"Told me to give you Kinsey's case."

Huh? "I thought Malloy asked you to look into that."

Will shakes his head. "Nope. Malloy doesn't even know about it."

"Well, shit." That means I'm technically going behind his back, doing work for another department. "You know I could get my ass in a jam for this."

Will lifts a shoulder. "Marcos said not to worry about it.

Anything comes of it, he'll back you up. Chances are pretty good that Malloy isn't going to get his undies in a bunch over us helping Kinsey, though. 'Course, if he was gonna get pissed at anyone, it'd be you, so. . . ."

Exactly. "Some bone you threw me, asshole."

With that, he gets to his feet and grins. "You have to start somewhere, Clark. Might as well be in the doghouse."

Kinsey

Still on for this weekend? I text Trent later Tuesday night.

You, me, and a bottle of lube?

Funny guy.

I try, princess. Want me to pick you up?

9pm?

One condition.

Ok . . . ?

Wear underwear. I won't be able to work wondering if you're bare assed again.

Ha! Just for that, I won't. *Promise.*

He doesn't respond, but it's just as well. Friday night is business and I can't go into it expecting more of what we did this past weekend. Granted, I wouldn't argue if he wanted to fuck me until I forget my name, but I respect that he has a job to do, too. So do I. If I don't figure out this mess with the missing inventory, corporate won't be happy. If corporate isn't happy, my job is at risk. I love what I do too much to take that chance.

Even if those few stolen minutes with Trent were the best I've had in a long time.

Shutting off the TV, I double-check the lock on the front door and pad barefoot to the bathroom for a quick shower. It's only seven o'clock, but I'm still beat from the weekend and a little reading before an early bedtime sounds fabulous.

When I'm done, I pull on a tank top and some shorts, then hurry to the living room to grab my phone.

Where my dad is sitting on my couch. With my phone in hand.

"What are you doing here? Again." I snatch the phone away from him and, sure enough, my text from Trent is lit up on the screen. Thankfully, I've listed him as Hardass in my contacts and our conversation earlier is the only one we've ever had via text.

"Who's the loser?"

"He's not a loser."

"Those texts are all about sex."

"I'm twenty-six, Dad. I have sex."

He cringes and I hold my head high. If he can pop the question without giving me the slightest hint, he can deal with the image of me twisted like a pretzel around some faceless guy.

"I heard you left with Sergeant Clark on Saturday."

I roll my eyes and hope like hell I don't start to blush. "We shared a cab." And a couple of orgasms. No biggie.

He narrows his eyes, then sighs. "I'm sorry I didn't tell you about the proposal. I wasn't even sure I'd do it there, but the moment felt right." He leans forward, elbows on his knees. "You said your mom would like Shelby."

"She would, Dad. It's not that. It's just . . ." I push a wet lock of hair behind my ear. I honestly don't know what bothers me so much about the new job and the proposal. Obviously, I wish he would have given me some warning, but it's more than that. Maybe the fact that we don't talk like we used to. A choice we've both made, so I can't blame it entirely on him.

"I know, honey." He gets to his feet and wraps his arms around my shoulders, kissing the top of my head, even though it's wet. "Let's do something this weekend, just the two of us."

"Um . . ." I'm pretty much booked up with work during the day and then the surveillance with Trent at night, both Friday and Saturday. "What did you have in mind?"

"Sunday brunch?"

Thank God. "Perfect." I squeeze him hard, reluctant to let go. "I'm happy for you and Shelby, Dad. She's an amazing woman, and it's obvious she makes you happy. Homicide, however . . . I didn't see that coming."

"I only have a few more years in me, Kins. I want to spend it doing something I love."

"You'll work with Will again?"

He nods. "Yep. Looking forward to it. He's one hell of a detective."

"He is," I sigh, rubbing my cheek against his polo. "But he's not my type, nor am I his."

"Why the hell not? He's a solid man. Good head on his shoulders."

He's just a little *too* solid. A little *too* straight. "He's not interested, Daddy. Every time you try to push us together, all you do is make it awkward for the two of us. He's a nice guy. I almost consider him a friend. I don't want to jeopardize that."

My father visibly wilts. His shoulders droop, his chin drops . . . his eyes lose their luster. "I've always imagined your future husband with a badge."

"Oh, God, Dad." I pull away, laughing softly. "Not me. Not even a little."

"What?" His eyebrows lift again. "You have something

against cops?"

"I haven't met a one that isn't completely stubborn. Present company included."

He grunts and his thick chest puffs as he inhales proudly. "Nothing wrong with being a little hard headed."

I tip my head to the side and smile. "So, you should be able to respect that I've made up my mind about this then."

His eyes narrow for a moment when he realizes I'm not giving in. "At least I don't have to worry about you and Sergeant Clark."

Um . . . "Daddy, please." *Please don't make me have to flat-out lie to you.*

He pushes a hand over his salt and pepper hair and sighs. "You sure you're okay with me and Shelby?"

"Absolutely."

Nodding, he twists his mouth into a nervous smile. "We've set a date. For next month."

"Holy crap." I blink up at him. "She's not pregnant, is she? I mean, I know she's younger than you . . ."

Dad tips his head back and laughs. "No, princess. We just don't see any point in waiting."

Shelby lost her first husband around the same time we lost Mom. I know she and Dad have bonded over those experiences and I'm so glad they've found each other, but . . .

Out of nowhere, it hits me . . . The reason I reacted the way I did on Saturday night. The reason I've been so unsettled since . . .

I've always thought of myself as an independent woman. I know what I want out of life and, for the most part, that's a solid, enjoyable career with a few perks along the way. A nice savings account, vacations, good sex . . .

I haven't done a lot of planning in regard to relationships, though. Settling down has never been a priority, and I realize now that it's because I've always had my dad. Since Mom died five years ago—when my dating life really began—he's been my rock. Him taking the next step with Shelby feels like that rock is crumbling. I guess I've known for a while that this would happen, but I never thought about where it would leave me . . .

Alone.

An only child with very little family beyond my father.

Not quite as independent as I thought.

"What can I do to help?" I ask, swallowing down the ball of emotion that's suddenly lodged in my chest. "Are you going big or small? Here in Vegas or someplace else?"

Dad gives a small, nervous smile. "Pretty small. Just family and a few close friends. We're thinking California. Napa."

Of course. Shelby's from northern California, after all. "That'll be beautiful this time of year."

"Will you be there, princess? Will you give me your blessing?"

"Dad . . ." His words hit me like a chilly gust of mountain air. They take my breath away for a moment, make my eyes water, too. "I wouldn't miss it for the world."

CHAPTER
Nine

Trent

BY THE TIME Friday afternoon rolls around, I'm done. Fried. Ready for a weekend of hitting the gym, watching preseason football, and drinking a couple beers. Why I agreed to scout out the Mile parking garage with Kinsey, I don't know.

Like Will pointed out . . . it's a bad fucking idea, but I let her frustration and helplessness get to me. Her asshole ex was giving her shit and she was—and still is—worried about her job.

I don't do personal, but I do fix things. I blame it on my mother, the quintessential do-gooder of our dysfunctional family. The more my old man screwed up, the harder she worked to keep it together. I sure as hell never wanted to be like him, so I guess I naturally took after her. Trying a little more every day to make up for his shortcomings. His crimes.

So, when I should be grabbing my shit and hitting the door, I take a seat at my desk instead. The station is quiet, with only a few of the second shifters hanging around and shooting the shit while the rest hit the streets for what's bound to be another crazy Friday night on the Strip.

I ran Tally Connor's background check earlier in the week and a quick review revealed some obvious red flags. If Chloe's Closet checks their employees before they're hired, they have a serious problem with their system. This girl is a train wreck.

A history of assault and battery, theft, and bail jumping a mile long, including two open felony cases in Reno.

Logging into Facebook, it doesn't take long to find her profile. She's set to semi-private, so all I can see are her pictures. Alone, she looks inconspicuous enough, but with her friends and all of their gang signs, she's not someone to mess with. Fortunately she's tagged a couple of her pals in some candid shots, so I grab preliminary checks on them, too. Interestingly, they each work along the Mile . . . and all three started their jobs about nine months ago.

"Shouldn't you be knocking on some poor woman's door right now? It's Friday night, you know." Will sneaks up on me, looking about as rough as I feel. Knowing he had a shit week makes me feel better about mine.

"Working tonight," I remind him, flipping through a few more pictures on Tally's profile. One image of her and a guy with neon green hair in front of the V Theatre catches my attention. They're mocking the Zombie Burlesque poster . . . and both are wearing skimpy ass lingerie. I screen shot the pic and send it to my phone. Maybe Kinsey will recognize the clothing . . . or lack thereof . . . as something from Chloe's line.

"Actually, that's why I wanted to talk to you." Will drops a stack of police reports on my desk. "We've had a few more reports of missing merchandise from stores in the Mile."

"Yeah?" I slide the reports closer, but the stores don't match up to the one's Tally's friends work at. I'm making assumptions, of course, and that's unlike me, but something about this whole mess screams bigger picture. But how and why, I'm not sure yet. "What do you think?"

"Could be related . . . or could be a fluke. We get these reports every day, so it's hard to say. I just thought I'd give you a heads up. Maybe you can check out the stores tonight before they close and then watch for any interesting behavior."

I nod. Nod a bad idea, just in case. "Anything ever come of your hotel homicides?"

"Some security footage showing the same woman entering and then leaving each hotel fifteen minutes later. Can't identify her though and somehow she only shows up on one other security camera. Same floor as the second vic, potentially around the time of death. No elevator footage, though. It's really fucking weird."

"Stats on this chick?"

"Tall and blonde. Stacked, too. I can send you a still shot next week." Will stretches his arms above his head and yawns. "I gotta get home, man. I'm running on two hours of sleep."

"New lady in your life?"

"Yeah. She's about seven pounds and has more hair than an 80's porn star."

I fold my arms behind my head and laugh. "A dog? You fucking sap."

"You couldn't have walked away either. You're a sucker for big brown eyes, too, apparently."

I don't even bother pretending that I don't know what—or who—he's talking about. "You gave me the case, asshole."

"Yeah, but I didn't tell you to plan a dinner and a stake-out with your informant."

He makes it sound like I'm not taking this seriously, and maybe I didn't at first. Then I realized Kinsey had a legitimate situation on her hands.

I want into Investigations. Hell, I've wanted to be a detective since I was a kid. I recognize the opportunity I've been given, even if it isn't major. It's still a theft case and there's an opening in the Metro Theft unit. I'm not going to fuck this up.

And yeah . . . I like Kinsey. It has nothing to do with what happened last weekend, either. She's a spitfire. She gives my shit right back to me, and I'm not used that. It's a damn refreshing change of pace, at least coming from a chick. Kinsey and I . . . we could be friends. She's sure a hell of a lot better to look at than Will and the clown posse.

I have several reasons not to screw this up, and I'm determined that nothing will stand in my way.

Kinsey

"HEY, YOU. HAVEN'T seen you on the floor in a while, especially not a Friday night."

Tucking a stack of new black and fuchsia panties into a vacant slot on the display shelf, I glance up to see Tally smiling from a few feet away. The stripe in her dark hair is teal this week and I notice she's pierced her eyebrow again, which is a violation of Chloe's Closet's corporate policy. Then again, so is stealing merchandise. I think I'll pick my battles.

"You know this is my therapy." I flash a quick grin of my own and move onto another empty slot. The small pile of navy lace I set inside feels amazing beneath my fingers and I hope that whoever eventually finds themselves wearing the pretty panties feels just as amazing.

"I do." She goes to work on another section of the shelf, rearranging colors and sizes for optimal exposure and shopping ease. "So you know about me and Ben, huh?"

Ugh. "It's really none of my business, Tally. He and I broke up a while ago."

"I should've said something. As a friend, telling you would have been the right thing to do."

Oh, honey, we are so not friends. "It's fine. Really." I mean, yeah, I cared a lot about Ben and I gave him almost a year of my life, but I think I always knew he wasn't the guy I'd spend forever with. There's power—and consolation—in that knowledge, although I won't deny being more than a little confused about his taste in women. Tally and I are nothing alike.

"Good." She smiles, but it's not an expression of relief. In fact, she seems . . . disconnected. Then again, who I am to say? I wouldn't have pegged her for the type to steal, so I clearly don't know her as well as I thought I did. "Are you sticking around for the evening or . . . ?"

Ah, now we get to the real reason we're having this heart-to-heart in the middle of the store.

"Oh, no. I just have a hair appointment in a half hour. No sense in going home just to come back.

Her grin is more genuine this time, and I'm not surprised. "Anything special you want me to do tonight?" she asks.

Not swipe any of these pretty new undergarments?

"Nah." I give her my best put-on smile and finish up the last of the restocking. "I'm sure you'll be busy enough."

Trent

AT A QUARTER to nine, I pull into Kinsey's parking lot. I could easily text her that I'm here early, but knocking on her door and making her panic is too tempting. I probably enjoy making the princess sweat more than I should, but I don't care. It's fun and I like seeing that spark of exasperation flare to life in her eyes.

An older woman is watering plants in the lobby when I enter the building, and she gives me a polite, albeit curious, smile. I get it. I'm a stranger and it's getting dark. She's smart to be cautious, and I don't want her to worry, so I take out my wallet and flash my badge.

"I'm here to see Ms. Malloy. A friend of her dad's. Any

chance you could let me in?" I ask, nodding to the security door. I could hit the intercom, but then I'd lose the full impact of my early arrival.

"Oh, of course, dear." She punches her code into the keypad—14435—and the door unlocks.

I pause for a moment, debating whether or not I should give her a lecture on her overly accommodating behavior, but then I remember the woman upstairs and the whole point of wanting to get here early in the first place.

"Thank you, ma'am. Be sure the door locks tight behind me, now." I wink and she flashes a sweet smile.

Taking the stairs two at a time, I get to Kinsey's third floor apartment quickly. She's probably going to wonder how the hell I knew which one was hers, and I welcome the confrontation.

She opens the door on the second knock and my plan to catch her off guard dissipates like rain in the desert.

Her hair is down. Long and dark and gorgeous as fucking hell. I instantly want to run my fingers through it. Stick my face in it and just breathe. Shit, I want to push her up against the wall and kiss her fucking senseless before I mess her all up again.

But I don't, because I shouldn't.

At least not right now.

"You're early," she says, with narrowed eyes, trying to hide the fact that she's checking me out. Nothing fancy about a pair of jeans, a T-shirt, and boots, but the way her gaze travels up and down my body makes me want to puff my chest. Maybe flex my biceps a little.

"Sorry," I lie. "You're a little overdressed for a stake-out, aren't you?" We both glance down at her fluttery, yellow dress and sandals, and I try not to groan out loud. Goddamn, those legs. Not only are they stunning, but I've had them wrapped around me. Spread open before me, too. I know what she's got to offer and, fuck, if I don't want it again. Right now.

"I like this dress," she explains, her tone unnecessarily defensive. I'm only giving her shit because I want her to know that I noticed her effort.

"I'm not complaining, princess. I'm just reminding you that hanging out with me while you're looking so hot might be dangerous. Know what I'm saying?"

"That you're a pig?" She makes a sour face, but there's a sparkle in her dark eyes. "Yeah, I figured that out a while ago."

Smart girl.

"You want to come in, Sergeant? I have a few things to finish up before we go."

Hell, yes, I want in. Those things she needs to do, though? Not happening.

As soon as she closes the door behind us, I press her against the wall in her little hallway.

She gasps, but hangs on tight as I slide an arm beneath her ass and lift her, pinning her in place with my hips. "We don't have time for this."

"The fuck we don't," I rasp in her ear, already sucking that sweet skin between my lips while her hands slide beneath the back of my shirt. "That's why you invited me in, isn't it?"

"No . . ." Her voice is coy and cute as hell, despite the way she gropes me like a starved woman. "I was just being polite."

"That was your first mistake," I chuckle, greedily dipping my fingers beneath the thin band of fabric running down her ass. "Never let a strange man into your place, Kins. Ever."

She groans when I graze her tight little pucker and then find her pussy, already so wet.

"I think you lied to me." Nipping at her lips, I steal a quick kiss. "Unless you have another explanation for being so fucking drenched."

Her pretty eyes glaze over as I do nothing more than tease her slippery slit. "I got myself off a few minutes ago. Knew I wouldn't be able to last the night if I didn't."

Well, imagine that. She really does know what she wants, doesn't she? "What'd you do?" I demand, gripping her chin and making her look me in the eyes.

"Vibrator." She swallows hard and licks her lips. "Maybe a couple of fingers."

She has no idea how sexy she is, does she? "Maybe?"

"Just two."

The mental image of her leaning back against her pillows with her legs spread wide manifests quickly, and I'm instantly hard.

"I want a taste," I growl before I carry her to the living room and lower us both to the couch. A second later, I'm on my knees before her, pulling her thong aside. "Ah, look at you, princess. So fucking pretty."

"Trent . . ." Her hands slide into my hair and her hips come off the cushion as I lean in and lick from the bottom of her pussy, all the way to the top. "How do you know what I need?" she moans. "How?"

Because we share the same fantasy, Kinsey and me. I blame mine on a fucked up need to prove myself capable of giving more than I take, and I don't even want to know where hers comes from. I won't make a claim on her outside of moments like these, but I sure as hell don't want to think about someone else fulfilling her dirty fantasies either.

"Don't know, princess," I say, sliding my hands beneath her ass so I can hold her to my face and lap up every bit of her honey. "But I don't think you really care, do you?"

Her fingers tighten their grip on my head when I tease the tip of my tongue around her clit, then dive in when she least expects it, giving her the full of my mouth. More of that *everywhere at once* stuff she likes.

"Yes, Trent, God, like that . . ." Shoulders pressed against the back of the couch, she throws her head back and grinds hard against my face. I should remind her that I'm in charge right now, but I love this good girl gone bad version of Kinsey and I'll be damned if I'm going to ruin the moment.

I do, however, pull away just long enough to ask, "You like when I suck on your clit?" and her answer is a long cry followed by a rush of sweetness against my lips.

Mmmmmm. Not only is Kinsey stunning when she comes, but she tastes like heaven, too.

I lap up everything she gives me, before I make my way up her body and kiss her. Long and slow and deep, making sure she tastes it, too.

"See how sweet you are, princess?" She shudders beneath me and I smile. "Now that I've tasted you, there'll be no more getting off without me, is that clear? You want to come, you come for me. I'm more than happy to oblige as long as that's my reward."

A pretty blush seeps into her cheeks and I love the potent combination of hunger and innocence in her eyes. "Be careful what you ask for, Sergeant. I like to get off daily."

Thank fuck for that. "Like I said . . . I'm happy to oblige." When I wink and try to steal another kiss, she pushes me off of her with a laugh.

"We're going to be late," she says, straightening her dress and fussing with her hair. "Maybe this will go fast and we can come back and finish what we started."

Sounds like a plan to me.

CHAPTER Ten

Kinsey

"WHERE'D YOU GO to college?" Trent asks from the driver's seat of his truck. We're parked in the row across from Tally's car, but down a few cars and hopefully out of sight.

"I'm a Rebel, baby." I shoot him a wink and pop an almond into my mouth before glancing back to the elevator. Fifteen minutes until Chloe's closes and we can finally see what Tally's been up to.

"What was your major?"

"Business and romance languages, and don't you dare laugh about that."

He does. Loudly. "That's one hell of a combination, princess."

"One was practical and the other was just for me. It's called balance."

Trent just shakes his head.

"Don't judge, Sergeant. You're cuter when you just go with the flow."

"Oh, yeah?" He kicks back in his seat, looking sexy as hell. "But for the record, I wasn't judging. Just trying to figure out why a smart girl like you never left Vegas."

Oh. Well, strike another brownie point up for Hardass. "It's actually not very exciting," I tell him with a shrug. "My mom died when I was twenty-one. I stuck around to make sure my dad would be okay."

Trent blinks at me. "He'd be pissed if he knew that, Kins."

Yeah, well, too bad. "It's not like I hate retail. I mean, I know that I could be doing more than managing a department store, but there's something powerful about playing a role, however small, in making women feel good about themselves. I guess that's the romantic in me."

Just like that, his doubt turns to amusement again, those eyes dancing.

"Oh, that's right—you know all about that, don't you?"

He winks. "I plead the fifth on that one, princess."

"Oh, that's original."

"What do you want me to say?" His grin slants to the side deviously. "That I know how good I am?"

"That's exactly what I expect." His honesty is what makes this thing between us so easy. "Don't make this weird. Just be real with me."

He makes a wry sound, and then rests his head against the back of his seat, eyes on the ceiling. "I know how chicks work, Kins. You're not any different."

"Excuse me?" I swing the back of my hand into his chest and he laughs again. "I don't expect you to call me in the morning, Sergeant. Or ever for that matter." I'll be the one who picks up the phone. Maybe he'll answer, maybe he won't.

Rolling his head to the side, his gaze locks on mine. "Don't you think you deserve better than a temporary fuck buddy?"

"I know I do," I say without hesitation. "But that's not what I want right now."

"Oh, really?"

"I can draw the line, Trent. Just because I wear pretty dresses and sell sexy lingerie doesn't mean I'm weak."

His grin stretches wide again. "Believe me, princess, I know."

"Good." I toss an almond at his face and he rolls his eyes. "Now let's talk about something else."

"Like what?"

"I don't know. Anything." As long as it's not my reasoning for hooking up with him, because I'm not sure I fully understand that either.

"Favorite movie?"

"Huh?"

"Favorite movie?" he asks again. "Don't overthink it."

"Zoolander."

He laughs so hard, the truck shakes.

"Keep on judging, asshole."

Instead, he snaps upright and flashes me the blue steel glare. And then I'm the one making the truck rock.

"What's so funny, princess? Huh?" Reaching across the console, he tugs on a lock of my hair.

"You!" The giggles keep coming until they turn into tears. Damn him. He's not supposed to be jaded *and* adorable.

"Told you I'm not always a dick." Winking, he takes a pull from his fountain Coke. "It's like a ninety/ten split. Maybe eighty-five/fifteen on a good day."

"Well, that's generous."

"I try, princess."

I giggle all over again, knowing I'm edging closer and closer toward dangerous territory, even though I just said that wouldn't happen. "Favorite football team?"

"Uh, the Broncos, obviously."

"Eww. And here I was thinking we might be friends someday."

"Let me guess—you're a Cowgirls fan."

"Damn right. America's team, baby."

He makes a face and sits back again. "Probably for the best that we're not friends."

"Eh. You're a cop. It'd never work anyway."

"You and that cop hatred. You got some unresolved daddy issues, or what?"

My jaw slacks open. "You did not just say that."

"What's your problem with law enforcement if it isn't your old man?" He crosses his thick arms over his chest and I get the first glimpse of a tattoo high on his bicep.

"My problem is that you're all a bunch of cocky, power hungry jerks."

"You see the hypocrisy in that, don't you?" He grins. "You're condemning the very thing you like most about me."

Sly bastard. "I never said I liked you." At least not out loud.

"You like my cock, princess. And my tongue, too. The way you scream my name pretty much gives away how you feel about me."

Cocky jerk, case in point. "Give me something more to go on then, Sergeant, if that's not all you want to be known for."

He narrows his eyes and I point a finger at him.

"Exactly. You don't want me—or anyone—to know the real you, so you pretend to be a dick to keep everyone away."

"That's me, Kins, not every cop in the Metro."

"Yeah, well, I'm not fucking every cop in the Metro, am I?"

"Getting to know me better isn't going to change the outcome of this, princess. When we're done, we're done."

I asked for honesty, but damn, that stings.

"There she is."

"Huh?"

Trent points toward the elevator, where Tally bustles out with her oversized purse. Sabrina, her coworker for the night, is right behind her and, for a few minutes, the two of them chat at the back of Tally's car.

"Purse looks full," Trent says quietly.

"Yep." I wonder which of the new stock she's stuffed inside

tonight. "God, I feel sick."

"You want to confront her?"

"Not yet." Sabrina's a good employee. I don't want to drag her into this.

We watch for another minute and then Sabrina heads off toward her car. Tally climbs behind the wheel of hers, too, and my heart sinks.

"Shit."

"Just wait. She could be unloading."

Maybe. But then she starts the car.

"There's still time to catch her, Kins. Just say the word and we'll go."

I know it's my call. He's only here to back me up in case things get out of hand, but it'd be so much easier if that weren't the case.

"I don't know if I can do it." Suddenly I feel like an idiot. How could I ever think that confronting her would be easier than fixing the camera system?

"I'll do it if you want."

I swing my gaze to Trent's. "You'll talk to her?"

"No, princess." His lips curl sympathetically. "I'm not on duty and I couldn't make any headway without probable cause. I mean the cameras. I can fix them."

From nice guy to semi-jerk to nice guy. He's good at keeping me on my toes, that's for sure. "She's sleeping with my ex."

"The maintenance dude?"

"Yeah."

"Ouch."

No kidding. "I'm not going to turn down your help, but you'll have to be discreet. Tally can't find out the cameras are working." If she does, I'm screwed. I'll have nothing to back up the missing inventory and the corporate office won't like that one bit.

Trent pulls in a deep breath as Tally backs out of the parking space and heads toward the exit. "One of the good things about those cocky cops you don't like?"

"What's that?"

"We can be discreet as fuck."

Trent

"I THOUGHT YOU had the day off," Travis gripes from my mom's couch while the NFL pregame plays on the TV in front of him.

"I did, but something came up." Something that's forcing me to miss the Broncos first preseason game of the year. Against the fucking Cowboys, no less.

"Like what?" Tristan asks from the recliner, where he's sprawled out, and looking rough as hell from the night before. Must've been a good night on the pole.

"Like something I can't tell you assholes about," I snap, more annoyed with myself than them. Waiting another day or two to take care of Kinsey's wiring wouldn't have been the end of the world, but no. The prospect of seeing her again—and probably getting her naked, too—had me saying sure. Sure, I'll come over, princess. No problem.

"Language," Mom reminds me with a smack on the ass as she saunters into the living room with a tray of snacks. "Maybe you'll be done before the game is over."

"Maybe." I take a sip from my travel mug of coffee and shrug. Even if I am, there's a slim chance I'll pass up sex for cheese and sausage and a few beers. Not when Kinsey's such a delicious high all her own. "Then again, I don't want to see you two crying when your precious Cowgirls lose, so . . ."

Trav flips me off, Mom shoots me the death glare, and Tristan gives a hoot of agreement. "Hell, yeah, man!"

Mom swings her glare toward him, adding a pointed finger. God, I love these goons. We're each a little screwed up in the head thanks to good ol' Dad, but that's what's brought us together like this, too. I don't know any other trio of brothers that gets together with their mom to watch Sunday football. Then again, I wouldn't want to. This is *our* thing.

"I'll see what I can do to finish up early." I head toward the front door, pausing to kiss Mom's forehead over the back of the couch. "Save some food for me."

She pats my cheek and Trav snorts, shoving a handful of chips in his face like a greedy kid. You'd never know he was the oldest, given his smart mouth and goofball attitude, but I suppose that's his way of dealing with everything.

Tristan was only three when all hell broke loose in our family, so he's had the luxury of growing up relatively normal, save the knowledge that our old man is locked away in a prison cell the next state over. All things considered, the fact that Tristan only takes his clothes off four nights a week for a bunch of horny women is impressive.

Sometimes I wonder if I'm the most fucked up of all, especially on days like this, when I throw everything I've worked so hard for to the side and give into temptations I have no business giving into. Today, that wicked enticement is spending the afternoon with Kinsey, knowing damn well I'm not in a good place and won't be for the next month.

Two weeks from now marks twenty-four years since my life changed irrevocably. The man who'd taught me how to hike a football and throw the perfect pitch turned into a monster. Maybe I'd always known he had a dark side from the way he pushed Mom around, but no one could have predicted he'd flip the way he did.

That's why I can't let myself get close to nice girls like Kinsey. Fuck, my old man is the reason I can't get too close to *anyone*. Instead, I'm stuck on the hamster wheel, testing myself over and over again, just to prove that I can control whatever demons might live in the shadow I cast.

I'm playing with fire, liking the time I spend with Kinsey, but I'm also a man of my word. At least, to the extent I can trust myself to do what needs to be done. I told her I'd help her out and I will. The trick will be to stop myself before taking more than she wants to give. Before I get selfish.

There's danger in being greedy and there's gluttony in my blood. The odds are stacked against me.

"Hey you," Kinsey greets me with a bright grin when I stroll into Chloe's just after noon. Her redheaded employee, Jana, waves from the other side of the store, where she's dressing a mannequin in pink and black lace.

"Hey yourself. Is this still a good time?" I hope I'm not fucking things up walking in with my tools. I put them in a shoe store bag, just in case.

Kinsey nods and waves me toward the hallway at the back of the store. "I told Jana you were coming. She's been here since I started, and I know she's suspicious of Tally, too."

"Ah, okay."

"Just as long as Tally or Ben don't show up, we should be fine." Kinsey closes her office door behind us, and I immediately drop the bag and pull her close. "What's this for?" she asks, sliding her hands up my chest as mine curl around her waist.

I don't know where the urge came from and, frankly, it scares the shit out of me, but I can't let her see that. I go the safe route instead. "Figured I'd save you the trouble of hitting on me and just cut to the chase."

Her eyes go round and that sweet smile stretches wide. "Well, aren't you accommodating today."

"That's what you keep me around for, isn't it?"

She begins to laugh, but I dip my head and kiss the amusement right off of her lips. Clinging to my T-shirt, she toes up and strokes her tongue against mine, giving back just as good as she gets.

She's feisty, this girl. Soft and sweet, but full of fire right down to the core. She nips at my bottom lip and the gentle tug of her teeth sends a jolt of desire straight down my spine. My cock stirs behind my fly and the need to own her *right fucking now* rushes in fast.

"I want you," she mutters against my lips, already working on my belt and zipper.

My head warns me to do the right thing and slow this train down, but my gut says fuck it. *You can't change the rules midgame, man. You told her you'd give her what she wanted, now man up and do it.*

The problem is . . . I want her, too. Way the fuck more than I should. It's no secret that wanting leads to desperation, and desperation leads to really stupid decisions made in a dark alley at night.

Stupid decisions a man can never take back.

"Please . . ." Kinsey's rubs the tip of her nose against mine, and something altogether different flares to life in my chest.

This girl trusts me. She trusts me a hell of lot more than I trust myself, and maybe . . . just maybe . . . I can give her what we both want without fucking it all up.

Reaching behind her, I lock the door.

CHAPTER *Eleven*

Trent

THE NEXT MINUTE is nothing but frantic hands and heavy breathing. Kinsey pulls off her cropped pants while I roll on the condom and then . . . *fuckkkk*.

She bends over the desk, presents her tight little ass to me, and I sink inside without hesitation.

"Ah, princess, that's good," I groan when I bottom out. Just two strokes and I'm buried to the hilt, because this girl is always ready for me. Like her pussy is made for my cock.

"Harder," she gasps. "I need to come."

"You telling me what to do, Kins?" Leaning down, I nip at her ear and snake a rough hand around to her tits. Thank fuck for her low cut top and skimpy bra, because two quick tugs is all it takes to expose her perky flesh to my greedy palm.

"Trent . . ." My name on her lips is the best kind of song. I could listen to her say it over and over again in that breathless pant that's a perfect mix of begging and bliss. She's like a shot of whiskey to my ego. Strong and empowering.

"Mmm, these are nice." Hammering into her from behind, I play in the front. Her nipples are already tight little peaks, and every time I pinch or flick, her pussy clenches around my dick.

I want to see them. Suck on them, too. Make her come with nothing more than my mouth. But fucking her like this feels too good, so it'll have to wait. Another day, another time. Maybe.

"Goddamn, you're on fire," I breathe against the back of her neck, as she takes my punishing thrusts one after the other. "Such a hot little pussy."

"Oh, God, yes. Like that . . ." she rasps, and I pound harder, driving my cock into her core until she goes off around me like the Fourth of July. Tremors and soft cries, liquid heat soaking my cock, begging for more.

Feeling Kinsey's body react to mine is a high I can't explain. I don't even care if I get off myself, though I know I will, because making her shudder is a rush all its own. Something I've never felt before.

I'm losing control with her. I don't know how or why, because I've been extra careful. But it's there, glittering around the edges of my vision like an ominous blackout. The harder I take her . . . the deeper I connect with her physically . . . the more I slip.

The scary thing—the really fucking terrifying thing—is that I like it. I like it a whole fucking lot.

Pressing my lips to her temple, I close my eyes and breathe her in, letting her sweetness permeate my head and my lungs. The pressure in my balls and at the base of my spine builds fast and then I'm there, blood rushing in my ears like thunder.

"Ah, fuck, baby . . ." One hand splayed across her chest and the other digging into her hip, I come, giving her everything I have and then some.

As sated as my body feels, I know in my gut that this can't happen again. Being with Kinsey tempts the beast that lives inside of me—just like it did him—and I can't let that monster surface.

I actually care about this girl and if I were to hurt her in any way . . .

Pulling out, I spin her around, cradle her face in my hands, and kiss her hard. *I'm sorry, princess. I thought I could play this game with you and keep you safe, but I can't.*

Kinsey's fingers creep up my chest, until they curve around my neck, holding me close. Her touch is so damn gentle. So damn soft . . .

She's too fucking good for me. Always has been and always will be, regardless of whether or not she has a wicked side, too. Her demons and mine aren't in the same league, not by a long shot.

"You okay?" she asks quietly, when I pull back. Her warm hands slide down my arms and those gorgeous eyes smile up at me, completely unaware of how fucking dangerous I am.

"Yeah," I say, clearing my throat and yanking up my jeans. "You?"

"Perfect. That was . . . intense."

No shit.

"Hey . . ." She grips my chin between her fingers and turns my face back to hers. Those brown eyes aren't smiling anymore. "What's going on in that handsome head of yours?"

"Nothing." I shrug if off and take care of the condom with a couple of tissues from her desk.

"Trent . . ."

Damn it, why does she have to sound like she actually cares? Like she's truly worried about my fucked up thoughts?

"Princess, I'm fine." I shoot a wink over my shoulder and toss her pants to her. "That was good. Unexpected, but good."

The frown between her eyes says she's not buying it, but she lets it go anyway. Ten minutes later, I'm on a ladder with my head and hands in her ceiling. An hour tops, and I'll have her cameras fixed, which means my time with Kinsey is officially on the downslide.

For her sake, I hope it goes fast.

Kinsey

TRENT BARELY SPEAKS twenty words to me while he fixes the camera wiring. I'd like to think he's trying to work as quickly as possible so he can get out of here before we get busted, but that doesn't explain the way he held onto me in my office. Or the strange—almost scared—look in his eyes afterward.

His outright claims of being an ass have been frequent enough that I've started to wonder who he's actually trying to convince—me or himself? Yes, he has some jerk-ish tendencies, just like I have my snappy, bitchy ones. But behind the badge, he really is a different man. There's so much more to him than meets the eye and the glimpses I've seen of that mysterious persona are intriguing. And incredibly, incredibly sweet.

I felt it today when he buried his face in my hair as he came. He kissed me like he was trying to prove something, and I'm not sure what the hell that is, because I already know everything I need to.

I like him, and I wouldn't mind if we started to have something more than just sex.

"All done," he says, turning my laptop around to show me that all four of the cameras are up and running. "Was an easy fix. The wiring to the main camera was fried and replacing that alone brought the system back up. I still went ahead and changed out the others just in case."

"Thank you." I want to kiss him and show him how much I appreciate the effort, but I keep my distance, because he's giving off that untouchable vibe again.

"No problem." He flashes a smile that doesn't meet his eyes while he stuffs his tools back into the shoe store bag. "You said she works on Tuesday?"

"Yes, and she closes up alone, so I think we'll get what we need."

"Good. Call me Wednesday morning and let me know. I'll come by and check out the footage and we'll go from there."

Outside, it's probably ninety degrees, but the climate between Trent and me has gone from desert hot to Canada cool in a matter of an hour. He won't even look me in the eye for more than two seconds and, despite knowing full well what we've been doing wouldn't last, this sucks.

"What do I owe you?" I ask quietly, reaching for the store's checkbook.

"Don't worry about it, Kins. I'm a public servant every other day of the week, might as well consider this just another part of the job."

Great. Just the category I want to be in. He doesn't want to be friends, and now I'm a fucking job.

Wrapping my arms around myself, I try not to be bitter. "Thanks again. I really appreciate it."

"Sure thing." He rubs a hand around the back of his neck and tips his head toward the door. "I'm going to head out. Call me Wednesday, okay?"

I can still feel his hands on me. I can still taste the hunger in his kiss. I can still feel him buried inside of me, giving me something that no one else has before.

And he's walking away like it never happened.

What's worse . . .

I let him go.

Trent

THERE'S STILL A full quarter left of the game and probably

enough food at my mom's to feed an army, but I can't bring myself to go back. I should, because spending football Sundays with her has been an unspoken tradition for the last twenty-four years. A way for the four of us to come together in solidarity, just like we did back then, when the cops hauled my old man out of bed with blood from the night before still on his T-shirt.

That afternoon wasn't the first I'd seen my dad in cuffs. It wasn't the first I'd seen blood on his clothes, either. Usually, it belonged to Trav or me, and sometimes Mom when Trav or I couldn't get between them fast enough.

That Sunday, however, the blood belonged to someone else. A woman named Susan, who my father apparently liked a lot more than he should have. Or maybe he hadn't liked her at all, but that mattered little to the drunken, stoned version of my old man who'd stumbled into that dark, Las Vegas alley.

I slow my truck in front of the yellow and light brown house, just like I've done hundreds of times over the years. The same stucco pot sits on the steps, full of bright pink and purple flowers and there are at least five sets of wind chimes hanging from the porch.

I smile, so fucking glad that, despite the shit my dad did to her and the crime he made her witness, she was able to find some sunshine again.

There's not a damn thing I can do to change the outcome of that night, but I try anyway, every single time I get dressed for work. *Every fucking day I wake up.* The memory of her battered face on the news won't let me stop.

The knowledge that I myself could be just as dangerous pushes me onward. Doing all I can to be a different man. For me, my mom . . . for society.

But I'm his flesh and blood, and there's not a damn thing I can do about that. He flipped like a switch and so could I. Hell, I like women, vulnerable and begging beneath me. I like the power I feel when they turn themselves over to me and let me take control.

I told myself that I followed Kinsey into the bathroom at Franco's so I could protect her from an asshole that might not be so aware of himself. So in control of his desires.

The truth is I followed her because I wanted her for myself.

Just like I want her now.

What she's given me isn't enough. I want to consume every pretty fucking part of her, so that no one else can ever have her.

She's made me selfish. Greedy. Hungry. Desperate.

With each kiss and with every sweet smile, she calls to something inside of me.

I have to walk . . . before I do something we both regret.

Kinsey

"I GOT THIS, Kins. Why don't you head home?" Jana takes a box of scented lotions out of my hands and holds them away from when I try to grab them back. "Uh uh, boss lady. You've spent way too much time here the past couple of weeks. Go do something fun."

"Like what?" My job is my life, I have the smallest circle of friends imaginable, and I can't stop thinking about Trent. Fun probably isn't going to happen today.

"Get your nails done. Go have a drink at the sports bar where all the hot guys are watching the game. Hell, go visit your sexy cop friend. He looked like he could use some cheering up."

Ugh. "No, no, and absolutely no." I'm not going to embarrass myself over that man. The fact that he knows my most personal weakness is humiliating enough.

"I thought you hated him."

"I do."

"You're full of shit."

My eyes snap up to Jana's. "No, I'm not. He might've fixed the cameras, but he's still a jerk."

"Maybe, but he's obviously not a *jerk* jerk. He's more like . . . a sweet jerk."

"Oh, my God," I laugh, picking up an empty box from the floor. "Maybe you're the one who needs to go home. Take a nap, maybe. Get your head checked."

"I've worked with you for six years now." Jana presses her lips together in a mollified smile. "I've seen you date lots of guys, including Ben, who was obviously wrong for you."

"Whoa . . ." I hold up my free hand and start to back away toward the rear of the store. "I am so not dating Trent."

"I didn't say you were, but the fact that you assumed that's what I meant says it all. You like him, and I'm pretty sure he doesn't mind your company either, or he wouldn't have come here today."

He likes my company when I'm without panties. Any other time, not so much. He's more or less said that very thing.

"Is this an issue because he works for your dad?"

"God, no." But that's another reason why I should take Trent's lead and let go. My dad would have a conniption if something more came of this little tryst. Heck, he'd go postal now if he knew we'd gotten involved.

"Good, because then I'd have to remind you that what your father wants for you and what you want for yourself . . . don't have to align. In fact, the only thing that should matter is that Sergeant Hardass makes you feel some kind of way. And he does, doesn't he?"

I flick another glance at Jana, and her all-knowing smile breaks me. "Damn it, Jana. This wasn't supposed to happen."

"That's what they all say, hon."

"I like him way more than I thought I would and I'm pretty sure the feeling isn't mutual."

"Did you ask him?"

"No!" My laugh comes out a little too loudly, giving away my schoolgirl nerves. Nerves I haven't felt since . . . since my very first time in Franco's bar, eight years ago.

"Go home and bake him some cookies."

"What?"

Jane nods in earnest. "Bake for him and then ask him out. The cookies will soften him up and give you the upper hand. Men . . . they can't resist a good chocolate chip cookie and he'll turn to butter in your hands. I promise."

"You're crazy."

"I'm also married, so what does that tell you?" Fluttering her left hand in front of my face, she cocks her head to the side.

I roll my eyes.

Bake Trent Clark cookies. *Pssshh*. She's out of her mind.

I wonder if I have brown sugar at home . . .

CHAPTER Twelve

Trent

THE MONDAY NIGHT crowd at Franco's is more raucous than usual and I'm annoyed as hell. Fucking Travis should've had his ass back from Reno two hours ago, but *nooo*. The bastard decided to make a pit stop at an auction, and now I'm stuck behind the bar, slinging beers and pouring shots for a bunch of needy pricks.

"Yo, Trent, can I get another Coors?"

"Hey, Serg, how about some Fireball?"

"You're not gonna pull me over when I leave later, are you?"

No, motherfucker, I'm not, but I can promise one of my buddies will.

Fucking hell, I hate this.

"Hang in there, kid," Bernie, an old timer who comes in every night for two shorties, flashes a toothless grin. "You're doing all right."

No shit. It's not like I haven't worked the bar before. I used to do it all the time when my Uncle Don owned the place. I gave it up when I became a cop and my tolerance for bullshit disappeared.

"Hey, man, can I get three bottles of Corona?" Chase, one of Tristan's stripper friends, leans in next to Bernie.

I'd rather serve him my fist and a knee to the balls for

touching Kinsey a couple weeks back, but I lift my chin and go in search of his drinks instead.

Damn it, only two left.

"Pete," I say to the big biker dude sitting next to Bernie. "Can you hold down the fort for a minute? I gotta grab some more fairy juice for the ballerina."

Pete grins and Bernie snorts. Chase puffs his chest and tries to act like he's tough shit, and I dare him to come at me with some smart-ass retort. I'd gladly show him to the door and kick his ass all the way there. Unfortunately, he keeps his mouth shut.

When I return from the back cooler, Pete's behind the bar and there's a woman with long dark hair in his seat. Her back is to me as she talks to Chase, and I'm annoyed all over again.

What the hell is it with this guy and chicks? Is there a certain stripper cologne he wears that draws them in or what?

"Hey, man, she wants a vodka cranberry, but all I can find is orange." Pete holds up the OJ container and shrugs.

"In the other cooler." I nod to the unit further down the bar and duck down to unload the Corona. When I stand, Kinsey's brown eyes blink up at me.

"What the hell are you doing here?" I snap, regretting it the second she flinches. She shouldn't be here, but there's no need for me to be a dick about it.

"I wanted to give you something." Lifting a red gift box from her lap, she slides it across the glossy wood.

"You should've gone around back." I take the box and stow it behind the bar, feeling like an even bigger ass when disappointment falls over her face.

"The door's locked," she says, biting her bottom lip as her fingers curl around her little purse. "You know what? I think I'll pass on the drink and just go."

Fuck.

"Kinsey, wait." I grab her arm as she spins toward Chase, who, in turn, gives me another death glare. "Dude, you'd better quit looking at me like that."

"You're the one putting your hands on the lady, man."

Goddamn, I hate this guy.

"She's my friend," I explain, and then to her, in a softer, less admonishing tone, "Can you please just wait?" I can't let her go without apologizing. And not just for snapping at her.

She eyes me for a moment, probably trying to decide if I'm worth the effort. To my relief, she nods, so I dig out my keys and pass them across the bar. "Head upstairs. Trav should be back soon."

Her fingers brush mine as she takes the keys and I shiver. Right there in front of the entire bar.

"Lock the door behind you," I say, shooting a warning glance at Chase. "I have another key."

She nods again and then disappears down the back hall.

Chase grunts. "Your friend, huh? She was in here a couple weeks ago, looking to be my friend, too."

My hands ball into fists, but it's one of Pete's that sails across the bar, nailing the stripper square in the jaw. He stumbles back a few feet, holding his face and cursing like a sailor.

Pete shakes out his hand beside me, grinning like a fool. "Better me than you, Serg."

Probably. "Thanks, man. Your next round is on me."

"Appreciate it." The big guy winks, then points to the red box. "So, what'd your lady friend bring ya?"

"I don't know." Probably some sort of "thank you" for working on her cameras, though I'm not sure I deserve it. I was pretty much a prick after I fucked her.

"She looked disappointed that you didn't open it."

"Yeah, I noticed."

"Probably took a lot for her to come in here and give it to

you with all of us roughnecks watchin'."

Ha. "Guess I haven't been properly schooled in gift etiquette." Hell, I'm not sure anyone other than family has *ever* given me a present.

"What are you waiting for?" Pete nudges my arm, and I get the feeling he was one of those kids who snooped before Christmas.

Down the bar, a patron raises an empty bottle and Pete stalks off to take care of him. Guess that's my cue.

Working the lid off the top of the pretty box, I pray to God there isn't a bunch of sexy lace inside. Not that I wouldn't like that a whole hell of lot, but I'd never live it down if one of these assholes caught a glimpse.

The second the lid pops free, the mouth-watering aroma of something sweet hits my nostrils and I grin.

Cookies. She baked me friggin' cookies.

Goddamn, I like this girl.

"What'd ya get?" Pete's back, leaning over my shoulder.

"Mind your own business, bro," I tell him, slapping the cover back on the box before I pull out my phone and text Travis . . .

Get your ass back here. I got better shit to do.

Kinsey

HE GAVE ME his keys and, more importantly, free reign of his place.

That has to mean something.

Right?

God, I'm such a sap. He practically bit my head off downstairs, yet here I am, looking for the silver lining like a silly teenager. Stupid, Kinsey. *Stoo-pid.*

Sighing, I take my first real glance around the tiny apartment. It's plain and masculine, like I imagine most above-bar living quarters are, but there are little hints of Trent all around. Boots and tennis shoes lined up neatly by the door, an empty beer bottle turned upside down in the sink, a T-shirt draped over one of the kitchen chairs . . .

I pick it up and bring it to my nose, inhaling as much of his familiar, citrusy scent as I can. Who knows what kind of mood he'll be in when he finally gets up here, so I might as well make the most of the chance he's given me. For all I know, it'll be for nothing, but that's the risk I take, I guess. Putting myself out there for a man who may or may not want to know me as well as I want to know him.

Putting the shirt back, I make my way into the living room. The TV's on but muted, a recap of yesterday's preseason football games playing across the screen. On the end of the couch, there's a pillow, a rumpled fleece blanket, and an overturned book. A sci-fi thriller, which makes me smile, because of course blood and guts would be Trent's thing. Wild and a little out there, but with enough reality to make a person wonder.

I take a seat on the couch and pick up the remote, mindlessly scanning channels when the door handle jiggles and then clicks, and Trent strolls in.

"Hey," he says, tossing his phone on the table and setting the box I gave him beside it. "Sorry to make you wait. Travis had some shit to do, so I had to cover."

"No worries. It's not like I let you know I was coming." I give him a sheepish smile, complete with a shrug. "If I'm honest, I wasn't sure you'd even want to see me."

"Kinsey . . ." he begins, pushing a hand back through his hair with a frustrated huff. "We can't keep doing this. I know I said we could, but . . . *fuck.*"

"Look, I know . . ." I get to my feet and try to push my

foolish smile a little wider. "I didn't even expect that first night, so the fact that you gave me more was just . . . an added bonus."

He laughs softly, scrubbing his hands over his face. "Babe, don't sell yourself short. You're not a woman who should be fucked in a bar bathroom. The fact that I ignored that . . ." Breaking off, he casts a painful glance my way. "I wanted something I can't have, princess. Plain and simple."

"What the hell does that mean?"

"You made me cookies, Kins." Jaw clenched, he gestures to the box on the table. "You might have a wild streak beneath that polished exterior, but there are no chinks in your finish. Not like there are mine."

"I am far from perfect!" And the fact that he's using that as an excuse just pisses me off. "We all have demons, Trent. Every freaking one of us. However, some of us choose to deal with them, while others pretend they aren't really problems at all."

"What?" His eyes narrow to spiteful slits.

"What are your chinks, Trent, huh? Can you say them out loud? Own up to them like I have mine?"

His face morphs from pinched and confused to red and angry in an instant. "Don't you dare. Don't you fucking dare."

"What?" I laugh, knowing damn well that I'm only taunting the lion. "You think I can't handle it? That I'm too fucking *perfect* to understand?"

He closes the distance between us in three steps and slams me against the wall between the living room and kitchen.

"You don't know what I'm capable of," he growls against my lips, nothing between us but the air we breathe. "You don't know what I could do to you. Right fucking now, princess, I could take it all."

"Do it," I whisper, his big body pressed so tightly against mine, making it hard to say more.

He laughs and then jerks my hands above my head, pinning

me in place while fire flashes in his eyes. "You'd like that, wouldn't you?"

"You know I would. I'm just not sure you have it . . . *oomph!*" All the air rushes from my lungs when he thrusts his hips into mine and grinds, the hard line of his cock pressing into my stomach.

"I could fuck you in a heartbeat, Kinsey, but I won't. Not like you want me to."

No. *No, no, no, no, no.*

"Things have changed between us . . ." He brushes his lips across mine and I open for him, letting him in, even as tears sting in my eyes. "I want you more than I should and it can't be like that."

Why not? Why. The. Fuck. Not?

"There's shit you don't know," he says, skimming his mouth to my ear and then across my jaw. His tongue feels like a hot brand against my skin, and I want more it. Down my neck, between my legs . . ."Shit that could hurt you, and I care about you too much to take that chance."

A sob bursts past my lips and he's right there, kissing it away.

"There's a reason your old man hasn't tried to set us up, babe. He knows I'm no good for you. He knows how dangerous I am."

"Tell me," I beg, finally finding my voice.

"Ask him, Kins. I'm sure he'd be happy to tell you all the reasons you should've stayed away from me."

"I want to hear it from *you*," I rasp, and his eyes flutter shut as he presses his forehead to mine. I have no idea what I'm asking, but I can feel the weight on Trent's shoulders. I can see the pain and conflict in the lines on his face. I hear how fast his heart beats in my own ears.

If he doesn't deal with whatever this is, it's going to eat him alive and, if what he says is true, it might consume me, too.

Right now, I don't care.

Tugging my hands free, I curl them tightly around his waist and press my face into the crook of his neck.

"Tell me," I whisper again. "Tell me who you are."

CHAPTER Thirteen

Trent

I HAVEN'T TOLD anyone about my father. Not friends from college or the academy, not anyone from the Metro, other than Dez and Will, who've been friends since junior high.

I've never told a woman I was involved with, though many have asked. Usually my resistance led to them finding out on their own, and then it was over, because no one wants a guy with my kind of baggage knocking on their door.

But I need to tell Kinsey. She deserves the truth, even though I know it's going to push her away. One way or another, she'll realize the mistake she's made and she'll be gone, but if I tell her, maybe I can keep her here a little longer.

Christ, the way she holds onto me. Like she'll never let go and I wish that were true. She's gotten under my skin and when I'm not thinking about all the ways I want to fuck her, I think about the shit I want to do with her. Like take her on a date. Buy her flowers and dinner, and then hold her hand. Maybe hit up a football game. Show her why she should be a Broncos fan, so we can outnumber my mom and Trav when I bring her home.

Fucking hell, I'm in over my head, and that scares the shit out of me.

"It's okay," she whispers in my ear as her hands slide up and down my back.

Her gentle touch and soothing voice numb the fear that aches in my chest, and I drop my head to her shoulder, sucking in breath after breath of nothing but her.

She presses a kiss to my neck, and just holds me. I don't know how long we stand there—seconds, minutes, an hour—but they're the most peaceful moments I've had in years, and I feel the bands of resistance slowly begin to tear inside of me.

"I'm sorry," I finally tell her, my voice cracking. "I didn't mean to scare you."

"I wasn't scared." She nuzzles closer. "I'm never afraid when I'm with you."

Jesus. "You might not feel that way for long."

"Not likely, but there's only one way to find out for sure." Toeing up, she presses a soft kiss to my lips. "I trust you, Trent. I promise you can trust me, too."

Yeah, well . . ."My old man's in prison, princess. Has been since I was eight-years-old." Not the most trustworthy family tree, but what can I do? It's the one I'm fucking stuck with.

She nods, never taking her eyes off of mine. "Okay. He must've done something pretty bad."

"Sexually assaulted a woman outside of a strip club."

Her mouth forms a little O, and I grimace.

"Not pretty, princess, but that's not even the worst part." I wait for another negative reaction, but she brushes her fingers against the side of my face instead.

"Okay," she says, wetting her lips. "Go on."

"A bouncer from the club heard her screaming and, when he tried to intervene, my old man drove a six-inch switchblade into his chest. He died at the scene, and my dad ran."

"Oh, God, Trent . . ." She throws her arms around me again, squeezes tight, and absolutely blows my mind. "I'm so sorry, baby."

I pull back and blink down at her, positive I'm imagining this. She's *comforting* me?

"The cops showed up at my house the next afternoon. Cuffed him in bed while my brothers and I watched Nickelodeon. I found his bloody flannel when I took the trash out the next day. Mom brought me down to the police station, so I could turn it in, and they gave me a pair of fake handcuffs."

Tears seep into her eyes and she does nothing to hide them or stop them from slipping down her cheeks. Just waits for me to finish.

"Your dad was one of the arresting officers, princess. He was also the cop I talked to that day at the station, telling him how and where I found the shirt. My old man had already confessed, so they didn't need the additional evidence, but your dad still patted me on the head. Told me I did a good job and that I'd make a great cop someday."

Her face crumples as she cries, and twenty-four years worth of weight slides off my shoulders.

"I'm a monster's son, princess, and you belong to a hero." The ache in my chest throbs all over again, but it's the most liberating feeling I've felt in a long time. "Your dad will never let us be more than we've already been."

She sucks in a shaky breath and lifts her tear-soaked gaze to mine. "One, I don't belong to anyone. Two, I decide my fate, just like you've decided yours."

"I—"

She interrupts me with a finger to the lips. "You're not him, and you never will be."

"You don't know that."

"Yes, I do," she says adamantly. "You're a protector, Trent. You've proven that to this city for years, and you promise me the same every time you touch me."

I don't know about that. "I'm selfish, Kinsey, and I sure as fuck don't want anyone else to have you. That's not protection, that's greed."

Kinsey

I THOUGHT I wanted sex. Just a few wild, mindless nights where I could turn myself over to someone else and let them own me, if only for a little while.

What I really craved was trust. A connection. Something deeper than I'd ever let myself have before.

Trent gives me that.

I don't know how it happened. Or why. I've always been attracted to his arrogant cop attitude, but the man behind the badge is ten times more appealing. He's real. He's damaged. And he has the biggest heart.

I know he's scared. I am, too. But I'm not afraid *of* him. I'm afraid that I'm falling for a man who may never realize how amazing he is. A man who may never accept himself enough to welcome how I feel about him.

"Do you realize how strong you are?" I ask quietly, brushing my fingertip across his lips. "How aware and honest and brave?"

He gives a shaky laugh and shifts his gaze from mine.

Gripping his chin, I turn him back to me, but he closes his eyes. "Look at me."

"Kinsey, come on."

"Trent . . ." I'm going to win this battle; I don't care how hard I have to work for it. "What's it going to take for you to let me in?"

"I've already let you in," he says, jaw clenched. "You just can't stay."

"Why not?"

"Because, damn it." He backs away, frustration etched in the lines of his face. "I'm not the kind of guy a girl bakes cookies for—I'm the kind she calls when she needs her hair pulled or her ass smacked."

"Well, then. I didn't know that guys who like sex had such distaste for baked goods. Guess you learn something new everyday."

"You know what I mean!" His face turns red and he spins toward the kitchen, hands in his hair.

"Actually, I don't." I follow after him, tug the lid off the cookies, and take a bite from one. "Because I like cookies, almost as much as I like it when you slam me up against the wall. Like you can't wait another second to have me."

He watches me from beneath his eyelashes, nostrils flaring. "This isn't funny."

"Oh, I know it's not." I take another bite, loving how his steely gaze shifts to my mouth. "We can be a bunch of different things all at once, Trent. We aren't limited to just one."

"What the hell are you talking about?"

"I can be your booty call and your friend at the same time. You can have both of those things from me."

"I don't want you to be my fucking booty call, Kinsey."

"Then tell me what you want me to be."

His eyes are on my mouth again, so I lick my lips, hoping it'll help him along.

"Maybe I want to take you out."

"On a date?"

His cheeks flush and his jaw ticks, but eventually he nods. "Yeah."

"I would love for you to take me out."

"Even knowing what you know?"

"Especially knowing that."

"Kinsey . . ." Something painful flashes in his eyes and he tips his head to the side, silently pleading with me.

If he won't listen to me, I guess I'll have to show him.

Putting down the cookie, I wedge myself between him and the table. "There isn't a single thing about you that I don't like. In fact . . ." My hand rises to my chest, covering the ache that's settled there. "Most of the things I really, really like."

He shakes his head, and I press my hand to the center of his chest, knowing that what I'm about to say will split me wide open.

I say it anyway.

"It's possible that I'm already falling in love with those things."

"Baby . . ." Trent's head drops to mine, hope and fear at war in his eyes. "You don't know what you're saying."

"I do." This time, I'm the one who pleads. "Let me love you. Please. I promise it won't hurt."

"It already does."

"But it's the good kind. The kind that comes with opening up. In trusting someone else." I tap my fingertips against my chest. "The kind you feel right here."

He lifts his hands and curls them gently around my neck. "Why would you want to love a guy like me, princess? Why?"

"Oh, Sergeant . . . why wouldn't I?"

Trent

"STAY WITH ME tonight." In all of my thirty-one years, I've never said those words to a woman. I can count on one hand how many times I've crashed at someone else's place, but I've never woken up with company in my own bed, and there's a reason for that. My space is my space, and when I need to breathe, I need to breathe.

Right now, I need as much of Kinsey as she'll let me have. If I'm lucky, my craving for her will at least be tolerable by morning. If not, we're both calling in sick. I don't give a damn.

"I'll stay as long as you want me to," she says, brushing her lips across mine. "Just tell me what you need."

"All of you," I rasp, the raw vulnerability in my voice so foreign. Being this transparent with someone is unchartered territory for me, but I know Kinsey's not weak. If she thinks she can handle my demons, I have no choice but to trust her. Like she trusts me.

"Okay." Her smile is so friggin' pretty. So real. Every time she shines that light on me, I swear it hits the deepest part of my soul, warming me from the inside out.

"Come on." Taking her hand, I shut off the kitchen light and TV, before leading her down the hall to my temporary bedroom. Another three weeks and the work on my townhouse will be complete, and then I can make love to Kinsey in a real bed. For now, we get Trav's old college furniture.

"Cozy," Kinsey says, when I click on the bedside lamp. "I would've pegged you for a black comforter kind of guy."

Chuckling, I kick my shoes into the corner, and then toss the ratty quilt from the end of the bed on the floor. "We won't be needing that."

"No?"

"Uh uh." Snagging her by the hem of her shirt, I pull her to me, tug the cotton over her head, and toss it next to the blanket. Her hair falls from a messy bun, spilling across her shoulders and down over the pillows of flesh plumping out above her bra. Black and lavender lace. Pretty sure I saw it on a mannequin in the store, but it's a million times sexier on a woman with real curves. "Fucking gorgeous," I murmur, palming a full breast in each hand and loving how quickly her nipple beads for me. "Haven't seen these yet."

"I know." Her hands do a little exploring of their own, sliding beneath the back hem of my T-shirt and slowing gliding up to my shoulder blades. "Can I?" she asks, gently pushing the fabric higher.

"Only if I can, too." The sweetest blush creeps into her cheeks when I lift my arms and let her undress me.

She gasps the second the shirt is gone, then her fingers and hot mouth are pressed against my skin, loving every inch of dark ink that covers my shoulder and bicep. I want my mouth on her, too, but I let her do her thing, working her way to my back, knowing the best part is yet to come.

"Oh, my God." She sucks in a sharp breath when she sees it and I drop my chin to my chest, grinning. "*Transit umbra, lux permanet*," she says, reading the script across my shoulders. "*Shadow passes, light remains*. I love it! Why didn't you tell me?"

"Figured you'd see it eventually. Wanted to enjoy the reaction."

"It's absolutely perfect." She continues on her journey, marking her territory with soft, sensual kisses until she's back in front of me. I could let her love on me all night, because Kinsey's touch is quickly becoming one of my favorite luxuries, but there are things I want to treat her to, as well.

"You good now?" I tease, and she laughs.

"For a little while."

"Thank fuck," I growl, quickly replacing her fancy bra with my hands and mouth.

"Oh, God . . ." Her head falls back when I suck a pretty pink nipple between my lips and roll the other between my thumb and forefinger. Her fingers drive back into my hair, holding on tight, as I work her until she's shaking from head to toe. "You're so cruel," she moans, and I smile against her wet flesh.

"Yeah? Why's that?"

"You know why. I'm going to come before you even get my pants off."

"Well, let me remedy that then." In less than thirty seconds, we're both naked and breathless. "Better?"

She nods, but her eyes are glued to my cock. "I don't think I can wait."

A low chuckle rumbles in my chest. "Such a greedy little thing."

"You've made me this way."

"Have I now?" Wrapping a hand around my cock, I stroke it from tip to root and back again, squeezing out a bit of pre-cum, as she watches with rapt fascination. "You want it?"

"Fuck, yes." Her tongue swirls around my cock before her knees even hit the floor, licking my jizz away like it's fucking dessert. She's so goddamn pretty with my cock in her mouth, stretching her lips wide, but I want a deeper connection tonight. I want to make Kinsey mine.

"Come here, baby." Hauling her to her feet, I slide an arm around her waist and lift her off the ground. Her mouth is on mine in an instant, and it's go-time. No more playing around. No more teasing.

Her pussy, already so fucking wet, slides against my dick as she rocks her hips, trying for that perfect friction against her clit.

"That what you want, princess? You want to come on my cock before I even get inside?"

She doesn't answer. At least not with words. Instead, she wraps her arms around my neck and rises up just enough to take me home with one quick glide.

"Holy fuck, babe . . ." All I can feel is Kinsey. Wrapped around my waist, my neck, my shaft . . . It's the most intense feeling, knowing there's nothing between us, physically or emotionally. I could live in this moment, connected to her in the most intimate way. Closer than I've ever been with anyone.

"Make love to me," she whispers, locking her dark gaze on mine, telling me without words this time that she has more faith in me than I ever have.

"Like this? You sure?"

She nods and that last band of resistance snaps in my chest.

I lay her down on the bed and I take a leap of faith.

I trust myself to be the man she needs. The man she wants.

The man I never thought I could be.

CHAPTER Fourteen

Trent

"FORGOT TO SEND you that picture last week." Will drops a grainy eight by ten image on my desk Wednesday morning. "Figured you must've been too busy playing cops and robbers with Kinsey to remember."

I flip him off with one hand and pick up the image with the other. "Ten bucks says this woman wasn't born that way."

"Huh?" Will comes around my desk and I point to the blonde's Adam's apple. It's not huge, but it's there, just like the dick she's probably got hanging between her legs. "Well, I'll be damned."

"I can see how you'd miss that." Leaning back in my chair, I wink. "I know you like 'em with a little hair on their chest."

"Fuck you, Clark." He smacks me on the back of the head, as Dez strolls in looking like shit warmed over. "What the hell's wrong with you?"

"Don't goddamn yell!" My buddy drops into his chair, and immediately yanks open a drawer, pulling out a bottle of ibuprofen. He downs at least six with a swig of coffee, then closes his eyes and groans. "Never," he grumbles, "and I mean never, go clubbing with Vanessa and her friends. They're crazy. Every last fucking one of them."

"Vanessa?" Will frowns, looking from Dez to me.

"Front desk."

"I could've told you that, dumbass. She's, what, twenty-two?"

Dez lifts a hand like it takes all of his energy and gives Will the finger. "Go back to where you came from, asshole."

Will chuckles and glances back to me. "I actually do have to run. Just wanted to get that pic to you, in case something comes up."

"Thanks." Hopefully, Kinsey will see something from last night on the cameras. I like spending time with her, but now that we're officially seeing each other, I'd like to wrap up this case so we talk about her panties, not the one's missing from the store.

Will makes a quick exit, and Dez moans and groans as he digs his phone from his pocket.

"Look at this shit," he says, thumbing around before he hands the cell over. "Have you ever seen anything like it?"

I grab the phone and . . . holy shit. "Is that Vanny?" With her lips wrapped around another chick's tit?

"Yep, and that's Gwen, her friend-with-benefits. They tried talking me into joining them, but . . ."

"But what? Gwen looks pretty hot with all that purple hair."

"She is. She's also batshit fucking crazy, so I passed. Wasn't sure I'd make it out with my dick still attached."

Snorting, I scroll through the next few pictures, each of them just as off-the-wall as the last, which surprises me because this shit isn't Dez's cup of tea. Used to be back in the day, but that was half a lifetime ago.

"Nothing wrong with cutting loose every now and again. Just don't let Captain catch you hung-over like this. He may be on his way out the door, but he'll still pinch your ass, and it won't be the kind you like either."

Dez grunts and reaches for his patrol keys. "I'm going to go park my ass somewhere and take a nap."

Not ideal, but probably for the best. "See you at five, man."

He grumbles under his breath and waves me off as my phone rings.

Kinsey.

I wait until Dez is out of earshot before I stick the cell to my ear. "Morning, beautiful."

"Hey, handsome. I think I've got what you need."

Hell, yes, she does. "You don't know how ridiculously hot that sounded."

"Yeah, I do," she laughs. "Now get your sexy ass over here so I can show you."

Kinsey

"HEY, SERGEANT." I lean up and give him a big smacking kiss as soon as we're alone in my office. "You got here fast."

"Missed you. In fact, I was hoping I could talk you into coming over later."

"Yeah? Why don't you come to my place and I'll make you dinner?"

Digging both hands into my ass, he lifts an eyebrow. "You cook *and* bake?"

"I can also grill a mean steak," I whisper, tossing in a wink for fun. "But keep that between us."

He groans and dips his head to my neck, taking a playful nip. "Be careful, princess, or I might request you feed me on the regular."

"I'm sure we could strike a deal. You know, I feed you, you fuck me . . ."

Trent pulls away, laughing. "Show me the footage before I find something better for us to do, princess."

Such a tease. I'll be sure he makes it up to me later. "Fine," I sigh. "This might take a while anyway."

An hour later, Trent pauses the footage from the front desk. "That's the second time that woman was in the store. Do you know her?"

"I believe that's Holly from the Nike store. She's one of Tally's friends."

"Last name?"

"Um . . . Bergan?"

Trent scribbles down the name and then pulls up a web page. It's a Metro PD site, but not one I've seen before, but that makes sense because he enters a login and some sort of database pops up.

"Should I be looking at this?" I ask, feeling like my dad's going to walk in at any moment and bust us.

"Eh, just close your eyes. I'll try not to cop a feel."

I slide my chair over instead. "Just in case."

Trent grins and then types what I presume is Holly's name into the system. "Holly Bergen with two e's. Petty theft less than six months ago."

Ugh. "Well, that's reassuring."

"Actually, it is, because Tally just stuffed extra merchandise into her bag. While she watches."

"Shit, I didn't see that." He rewinds the footage and, sure enough, there it is, plain as day. "I didn't even pick up on Holly," I explain, feeling like a putz. "I was more concerned about the couple that comes in next."

Trent cocks an eyebrow and hits play on the laptop. The second the couple appears on the entrance monitor, he sits up a little straighter. "You've got to be kidding me."

"What?" I lean in, but he just shakes his head and keeps watching.

The couple works their way around the store, popping up sporadically on each of the cameras. The man, a tall, lanky guy, keeps fondling the new pink and black corset Jana put on a mannequin last weekend. Before long, Tally approaches and the two of them exchange a few words, though the cameras don't pick up any sound. When he rejoins the other woman, Tally takes one of the corsets hanging on the rack back to the cash register.

"She couldn't possibly make it any more obvious," Trent says a few minutes later, after Tally and the man do the same thing with more elaborate pieces, at least a half dozen times.

"Who is he, do you think? I don't recognize him at all."

"Long story, but I'm going to guess the shit he's taking is for his own personal use."

"Really?" I guess you never can tell.

"Yeah, but she's pretty interesting, too." He nods to the woman he came in with, who keeps moving around the store, idly checking things out. Only once did I see her stuff a pair of panties into her pocket, but Trent watches her closely, his brow furrowed.

"What are you thinking?"

He leans back in the chair and scrubs a hand over his bristled jaw. "I'm thinking we've got a bigger problem on our hands than we anticipated."

I don't like the look on his face one bit. "Such as?"

Huffing out a breath, he hits a couple buttons on his phone and pinches the bridge of his nose. "Dez, wake your ass up. I need you at Chloe's Closet ASAP."

Trent

"SEE? I TOLD you she was nuts." Arms folded across his chest, Dez shakes his head at the images on the computer screen. "I don't know who the guy is, though. I don't recall any dudes from last night."

"That's not saying much, man. All those tits in your face, I'm surprised you remember your fucking name." I glance from my coworker to Kinsey, who's pacing a groove in her office floor and chewing her fingernails like a goddamn beaver. "Babe, sit down. Please."

"I knew this was bad," she says, still traipsing back and forth. "Damn it, I should've had the cameras fixed sooner."

"Babe?" Dez asks belatedly. "What the hell am I missing?"

"Nothing," Kinsey and I say at the same time, and Dez's eyebrows fly toward his hairline.

"Well, then," he mutters. "Someone's gonna get his ass chewed and, surprise, surprise, I think that someone is you, Clark."

"Shut the fuck up and concentrate," I snap. I know he's not going to rat me out, so I'm not worried about it. I am, however, concerned about this lingerie stealing bastard on the screen. "Are you sure the girls didn't have any male friends? Or maybe a friend in drag?"

"I don't know, man. I got a weird vibe from Vanny's friend, Crystal, but I'm positive her rack was real."

"How positive?"

"Firm C cups positive."

Jesus fuck. "You felt her up?"

"She offered."

"Did she ask you to suck her dick, too?"

Dez's face goes red and his nostrils flare. "No fucking way."

"We're going to have to bring Vanny and her girlfriend in.

We need this guy's name." The sooner the better, too, because if this guy is our hotel killer, he just stocked up on new lingerie.

"What about Tally?" Kinsey asks, biting her lip nervously.

"Tally, too." I nod. "We're going to have to move fast, because if this guy finds out we're looking for him, he could run. Kins, I want you to pack it up and get out of here. Just in case word gets around and he or Tally come here, pissed off."

Her eyes go wide. "You think that might happen?"

"No, but I want you at home anyway. Where I know you're safe."

"Oh, God." Panic washes over her face and I round the desk, pulling her against my chest.

"Just work on that amazing dinner you promised me," I say into her ear, rubbing reassuring hands up and down her back. "I'll be there as soon as I can."

She nods and presses a sweet kiss to my cheek. "Be safe, handsome."

Kinsey

AS SOON AS he downloads what he needs from the surveillance system, Trent walks me to my car, promising to let me know when Tally's been brought in.

I stop by the grocery store and make a quick run through, grabbing what I need for dinner and dessert. I snag some wine and Guinness, too. I haven't had a man in my apartment for any length of time since Ben, so I'm woefully unprepared for entertaining.

Except for clean sheets. I absolutely made sure I had those, just in case Trent's in the mood for a sleepover after what is sure to be one hell of a day. Maybe I can talk him into a bath. Or a blow job. Or both.

God. He's dealing with some serious crap right now and all I can think about is getting him naked. What is wrong with me?

Setting the gutter brain aside, I get home and haul my loot upstairs. I'm just unloading the wine and beer, when the buzzer sounds, which is weird as hell, because I'm never home during the day.

Thankfully, the intercom system has a camera and I highly doubt if someone—like Tally—were to show up and want to kick my ass, she wouldn't ring my bell . . . *before* she rang my bell.

I hurry around to the intercom and seeing Shelby in my lobby is probably more surprising than if Tally had shown up.

"Hey, Shel, come on up." I buzz her in and then wait by the door while she makes her way up the stairs.

"Hi, sweetie," she says with a big smile. "I was in the neighborhood and saw your car in the lot. I hope you don't mind that I stopped."

"Of course not. Come in."

Kicking off her sandals, she follows me to the kitchen in her bare feet. Her toes are done up in a hot pink color that matches her lips and goes perfectly with her California blonde hair.

Physically, she's the exact opposite of my earthy, flower child mother, who'd always worn her hair in a loose braid without out a stitch of makeup on her face. Both women are beautiful in their own way, inside and out, and my dad is one heck of a lucky guy to have found both of them.

My gut tells me that someday I'm going to look back and feel the same way about Trent. He's unlike any other men I've dated, and all too easily, I can imagine my future with him.

"Oh, you were shopping." Shelby smiles and begins helping me put things away. In my little kitchen, it's not hard to figure out where things go. "If I didn't know better, I'd say you were expecting company."

"I am." I'm not sure where the urge to confess comes from, but it feels right. My mom passed when I was twenty-one. I've never had the luxury of talking about my love life with her—at least not beyond the goofy teenage years.

Shelby's eyes light up as she tucks the ricotta and mozzarella cheese into the fridge. "Yeah? May I ask who he is?"

Moment of truth. I know damn well she's going to tell my dad, but I'm not sure I care. I'm not ashamed about seeing Trent, even if Trent himself isn't as sure. He's a good man, and I'm intent on making him believe it.

"Sergeant Clerk," I tell Shelby. "You may have met him at the PD ball."

Her mouth falls open, but her eyes are nothing but twinkling stars. "Kinsey Malloy, you're dating an officer?"

I nod and slide the pasta sauce into the cupboard. "It's only been a few weeks. We're . . . taking it slow." More like going backwards—sex first and getting to know each other later—but I keep that to myself.

"So, you'll bring him to the wedding, then?"

A weekend in Napa with Trent and my dad? "Um . . . maybe?"

Shelby claps her hands together with a squeal. "This is wonderful!"

"You think so?"

"Yes!" She throws her arms around me and sighs. "I want you to be as happy as your dad and I are, sweetie. You deserve someone strong and brave, and I can't think of anyone better for you than Trent."

"Do you think Daddy will approve? I mean, I'm not going to stop seeing Trent if he doesn't, but . . ." I'd kind of like it if my dad didn't disown me.

"It doesn't matter if he approves, Kinsey." Shelby pulls back and smiles. "Only your heart can decide who you fall in love with."

CHAPTER Fifteen

Trent

"YOU HAVE THE right to remain silent. Anything you say can and will be used against you in a court of law . . ." I slap the cuffs around Tally Connor's wrists, finish reciting her rights, and hand her over to Dez, who hauls her out of the apartment, right behind Gwen Martinez.

Christopher VanGaard, otherwise known as a drag call-girl Crystal Vee, lies face down on Tally's living room floor, foaming at the mouth with rage.

"I want my fucking lawyer," he roars, spit dripping down his chin. "I didn't have any part in stealing that shit from the mall!"

"The mall is the least of your problems, buddy." Will hikes the guy off the floor with a bored sigh. "We found your DNA at the scene of a murder, too. On a pair of panties."

"Yeah, but I didn't kill that guy, man! I was only there to party!"

"With knives and lingerie? Shit, dude . . . that sounds like a fucking circus act."

"That's exactly what it was!" The perp's eyes go as round as his fake tits. "It's what I do! It's one of my package deals!"

Will bites his lips together and I shift my gaze to the floor, knuckling my nose. I can't look at this guy without seeing Dez feeling him up. Lucky for Dez, Crystal doesn't recognize him, which I'm sure Dez wishes were the case for himself, too.

"Enough chit-chat," Will says. "You can tell me all about your packages down at the station." Rolling his eyes, Will escorts the creep out, leaving me with Chief Deputy Marcos and Detective Rusk.

"That went hella fast," Rusk says. "I never expected we'd find them all here."

"We owe that to Vanessa," I tell them both. "Though she's not happy about ratting out her girlfriend."

"I don't think Purple had much to do with this mess," Marcos says, glancing around at all the stolen loot stacked in Tally's living room. Shoes, electronics, goddamn essential oils . . ."But that remains to be seen, I guess."

"Ian, you want to head back to the bedroom and grab a couple more pictures of the things in the closet before we have someone come in and bag all of this?"

Detective Rusk nods and heads for the back hall.

"Definitely not how I saw this one panning out," I say, scratching my jaw. I'm pretty sure Marcos didn't either, or he wouldn't have put me on the case.

"Yeah, that's how it usually goes, though." The older man grins. "We do live in Vegas, Sergeant."

"True enough," I laugh. "Thanks for the opportunity, by the way. Definitely not a case I'm likely to forget."

"Well, I'd hope not, Sergeant. In fact, I expect you to rehash every detail next Tuesday when you meet with Transfer Committee."

Uh, what? "Excuse me, sir?"

Marcos blinks at me. "The Transfer Committee."

Um . . .

"The job's probably already yours, since Captain Malloy put a good word in for you, too, but you still have to go through the channels. Protocol is protocol."

Holy shit. "I'm sorry, Captain, but I'm unclear exactly what's happening next Tuesday."

Marcos looks at me like I'm crazy. "What do you think I'm telling you, Sergeant? Next Tuesday. Have your ass at HR for your Investigations interview. What's so hard to understand about that?"

I can't keep the grin from stretching across my face. I know I look like a dorky kid who just scored his first date, but that's sort of what this feels like. "You got me an interview?"

Marcos lifts a shoulder. "Nah, Captain Malloy's responsible for that, but you didn't hear it from me."

I can't believe what I'm hearing. I just . . . wow.

Kinsey's dad—the cop who's given me hell for years—went out on a limb for me. Knowing every gory, dysfunctional detail of my family history didn't matter. He still stuck his neck out there . . . for the little boy with the plastic handcuffs.

Holy fucking shit.

Kinsey

SALAD? *CHECK.* LASAGNA? *Check.* Strawberry shortcake? *Check.*

New garters and a G-string? *Check. Check.*

Waving a hand in front of my face, I blow out a breath and try to calm my nerves. I've been sleeping with this man for weeks. He's seen—and tasted—virtually every part of my body. Feeding him actual food should be a piece of cake, except it feels like I'm sharing my deepest, darkest fantasy with him all over again.

What if Italian isn't his thing? What if he's allergic to

strawberries? What if one of my garter clips snap and takes out his eye?

God.

I close my eyes and pull a breath through my nose, then push it out through my mouth.

And then my buzzer rings, making my heart skyrocket all over again.

"Come on up," I tell Trent, taking a moment to fuss with my hair in the hallway mirror before I meet him at the door.

"*Pheeew,*" he whistles when he hits the top of the stairs. "Look at you, all dolled up."

"This old thing?" Batting my eyes, I flip the hem of my new dress coyly. I bought it as backup for the PD ball, so it's probably a bit much for dinner at home, but it's pretty and I know how much Trent likes easy access.

"You look good enough to eat." His stubble scratches against my jaw as he dips to my neck and takes a nibble. "So does whatever you've cooked."

"Just lasagna."

"I fucking love lasagna," he says, finally kissing me properly, while I give a mental fist pump.

"I figured you'd be starving after the day you've had."

"Eh." He lifts both shoulders and closes the door behind us. "It actually went pretty smoothly. Vanessa told us exactly where we could find them. I think she's officially freaked out, realizing the kind of company she's been keeping."

"What about Ben? Did anything turn up on him?"

Leaning in the kitchen doorway, Trent eyes me carefully. "Actually, yeah. He was at Tally's, too. Will took him downtown for questioning."

"Oh, my God." My stomach suddenly whirls with . . . I don't even know. Disgust? Shock? Embarrassment?

"What's going through your head?"

I open and close my mouth, not entirely sure what to say. "I . . . I guess I'm kind of speechless."

"Because you still have feelings for him or because you didn't see it coming?"

My gaze flies back to Trent's and the uncertainty in my gut quickly becomes an ache in my chest. "I don't have feelings for Ben."

"You sure?"

"Absolutely." I turn away, reaching into the cupboard for wine glasses when Trent sneaks up behind me, slipping his arms around my waist.

"Then why are you freaking out, princess?" His scruffy cheek presses against mine and I close my eyes, letting myself enjoy the moment before I potentially ruin it by coming clean.

Turning carefully in his arms, I lock my eyes on his. "I want us to always be honest with each other. About everything. Even if it seems trivial or silly."

"Okay." His brow bunches as he nods. "But where's this coming from?"

Smoothing my fingers over his shirt, I rub away invisible lines, trying to come up with the right words. I've already hinted at the L-word, but talking about the future so early in our relationship is terrifying. I don't want to scare him off with too much, too soon, but I don't want to risk losing him by not sharing enough, either.

"I haven't always been so open about what I want," I admit quietly. "Or what I need."

"I think you've done a pretty good job so far." He brushes a strand of hair behind my ear, letting his fingers linger. "Unless there's something else."

Just say it, Kins. Tell him. "I don't want us to date anyone else. I . . . I never felt about Ben the way I feel about you."

A slow smile curls at one side of his mouth, and I can't tell if he's laughing at me or with me. "Are you asking me to go steady, Kinsey Malloy?"

"No! I mean, yes. Kind of. You know . . . if you want to." *Smooth, Kins. Where's your 'check yes or no' note?*

"Yeah, I don't know about that." He sticks his tongue in his cheek, gives his head a brief shake, and my stomach drops to my toes. "Would I have to hold your hand? Open doors? Kiss you goodnight?"

"Um . . ." My face is on fire and I haven't even opened the wine. "If you wanted to?"

Stepping back a bit, he studies me carefully. "Are those things you want, too?"

"Maybe?"

"Hmm."

"I'd also like you to come to California with me in a few weeks. For my dad's wedding."

"Already? That was fast."

"Malloys don't do it any other way, apparently."

He chuckles, flashing another killer grin. "I've noticed, but you know what? I dig it."

"Yeah?" *Does that mean . . . ?*

"The only problem I see with this arrangement is that if you keep baking and feeding me, I'll get fat. Probably going to need a lot of sex to keep in shape."

"I'm game for that. Definitely." Hell, I'd be up for anything he suggested.

"How about we eat so we can get to working out? Then we can talk about all the ways we'll burn off those wedding cake calories." He waggles his eyebrows and I laugh. From hardass to my hunky, horny man. I love it.

"You're asking for trouble, Sergeant."

"You think I'm afraid of your dad? *Psshh.* He's the least of my concerns."

Trent

"GODDAMN, THAT'S GOOD." Arms wrapped around her waist, I flick my tongue against Kinsey's tight, little nipple, loving the slow and steady way she rides me. Fucking her hard and fast blows my mind, but making love to her like this? I could do it every damn day.

"*Ohhhh,*" she moans, her head thrown back with that mess of dark hair spilling down her back like a goddess. "I could get used to—"

Suddenly, she gasps and goes stock-still.

"What's wrong?" I pop her nipple from my mouth and flex my cock inside of her. Whatever it is can't be nearly as important as finishing what we've started.

"I thought I heard the door."

"I locked it when I came in."

"Yeah, but that won't stop—"

"CLARK!"

"—my dad."

Fuckkk.

EPILOGUE

Kinsey

"AW, YOU GUYS!" I pull Dad and Shelby in for a hug as the warm California breeze ruffles through my hair. Early fall is rich in the air and, on the other side of the open pavilion, the band plays a sappy, instrumental 80's ballad. "Today was absolutely perfect."

Shelby laughs softly in my ear and Dad's hand rubs up and down my back. "Thank you, princess. It means so much that you spent the day with us. You and . . . Sergeant Clark," he says, his tone turning gruff on the last two words.

In the three weeks since he burst through my bedroom door like a raging bull, his feelings about me dating Trent haven't changed much. Even when Shelby invited us to dinner, Dad spent more time staring daggers at Trent than he did anything else. Never have I know my dad to be so . . . *opinionated* about my choice in men.

The interesting thing is that I know he actually really likes Trent. Despite all the crap he's given him over the years, Daddy gave him a glowing recommendation for the Investigations transfer. I can't even think about it without getting choked up, but suffice to say that my dad never forgot the brave little boy who came into the police station that day twenty-four years ago. There's a bond there that I'm not sure I'll ever fully comprehend and that's okay. I don't need to, as long as the two of them appreciate its significance.

The problem, however, is that that little boy turned into a man who's seen Daddy's princess naked.

No bond in the world would ever make that okay, at least in my father's eyes.

Detangling from the group hug, Shelby hurries over to Trent who lingers patiently behind us looking so handsome in his suit and tie. She throws her arms around him, too, and I laugh at his wide eyes and awkward acceptance. Dad grunts.

"Come on, Daddy. He's not so bad."

Dad shoots me a hard look and all I can do is smile.

"It's your fault you saw what you saw, you know. I told you to stop breaking in."

"And you told me it was just a cab ride."

I suppose I did, but I have no regrets. These past six weeks with Trent have been incredible. Minus the fact that he pulled me over *again* last week. Said it looked like I wasn't wearing my seatbelt, so he took it upon himself to make sure I was properly secured, complete with a full, second-base groping session.

"Only two more weeks of patrol, princess. Gotta make the most of it," he'd said before winking and heading back to his SUV like he didn't just get me all hot and bothered on Flamingo Road.

"Can we have a minute alone?" I ask my dad, who eyes me warily. "Just a minute or two. I won't keep you from your new bride for too long."

We make our way outside the pavilion and into the shadows. The sky is so clear, its millions of stars shining bright. I have to think that one of them belongs to Mom, smiling down on us tonight.

Looping my arm through Dad's, I sigh. "She'd be so happy for you." I can't bring myself to say more without falling apart and, given Dad's silence, I know I don't need to. He's thinking about Mom, too.

After several moments of walking casually toward the vineyard, he finally speaks. "She'd be happy for you, too, princess. Just like I am."

"Really?" I turn to him, surprised.

"Yeah." He nods slowly, his hands squeezing gently around mine. "He'll be the one to take you from me, Kinsey. I see it in his eyes."

"Dad," I laugh, a sneaky tear sliding down my cheek. "That's not a bad thing, is it? You have Shelby now. You can't expect me to be alone forever."

"No, but I've enjoyed being your number one guy all of these years." Emotion glints in his gaze as he smiles down at me. "If I could stop time, I would've done it years ago, princess. But that isn't possible and whether or not I like it, you've grown up. You've made me so proud. You know that, don't you?"

More tears fall, but I can't stop from smiling through them. "I know, Dad. I'm proud of you, too. We've done good, the two of us."

"That we have." He pulls me in, and I close my eyes as I rest my head against his chest. We stand like that for a long moment, before he asks, "He's your guy, isn't he?"

"Yes." The answer comes easy. I think I've known since that first night above the bar. "I know he's not the man you saw me with, but—"

"Honey . . ." Dad leans back and shakes his head. "The only thing I've ever wanted was for you to find someone who would love you as much as you deserved. Someone who'd stand up for you and fight for you."

Trent's fought all of his life. Mostly, he's battled his own demons, but, besides my father, there's no one I trust more to go to bat for me. I'd do the same for him in a heartbeat, too.

"Trent proved to me what kind of man he is years ago and, even though I didn't appreciate finding the two of you like I did, he proved it to me then, too. He could've been a coward. He could've run out the second I came in, but he didn't." Dad pauses to chuckle, and I blush, remembering that all too awkward confrontation. "He holds his chin high wherever you're concerned, and I have to respect a man who won't back down."

Me, too, though I know it doesn't always come easy for Trent. I have no doubt how he feels about me, but he's definitely his own worst critic. Feeling like he's enough for me is a daily struggle, but I'm more than willing to let him show me . . . over and over again, as often and as hard as he needs to.

"I think he's going to be around for a while," I say quietly, smoothing down the lapels of Dad's jacket. "Because I don't plan on letting him get away."

"Ah, hell . . ." Dad tips his head back and lets out a full-bellied laugh. "I'm not sure I'll ever get used to you being a grown woman, Kinsey Grace. Not in this lifetime."

"You realize I've been grown up for about eight years now, right?"

"Yes, but this is different." He's suddenly serious again. "You know it just as well as I do."

I can't argue with that, not one bit. My heart tells me it's true every time I look into Trent Clark's blue eyes.

Trent

"TODAY WAS SO beautiful." Walking barefoot in the grass ahead of me, Kinsey spreads her arms wide and spins in a slow, blissful circle. Her hair whirls around her shoulders and the hem of her dress lifts in the air just as carefree as she looks in this moment.

"It was nice," I agree, with her heels dangling from my fingers. "I'm glad you asked me along."

She stops a few feet from the cobblestone pathway that leads to our private quarters, overlooking the vineyard. The light glowing outside the door sets one side of her face in shades of gold, while her eyes sparkle beneath the California moonlight.

"Of course, I'd ask." She smiles softly, but there's hesitance in the expression. Uncertainty. "You know I wouldn't want to be here with anyone else."

"Likewise," I tell her, stopping only when I'm close enough to feel her breath on my face. "What's wrong?"

"You said that like I did you a favor, asking you to come."

"Well, yeah." I lift a shoulder, trying for casual, though I'm anything but. I've waited all damn night to get her alone. "You kind of did, didn't you?"

Her pretty red lips part and her eyes search mine frantically. "Baby . . ."

God, I love when she says that. Almost as much as my name on her lips when she comes. "What?" I ask, playing dumb.

"Ugh!" She shoves at my shoulder and spins toward our room, but I'm faster, dropping her shoes so I can catch her by the waist.

"Where you going, princess, huh?" Her sweet perfume fills my nostrils and I bury my face in her hair, breathing deep.

"You know I wanted you here!" she protests, stomping a little foot into the grass. "God, Trent, sometimes I don't know what else I have to do to—"

Spinning her around, I crash my mouth to hers, turning her frustrated words into soft moans. When her hands slide into my hair and her body goes limp in my arms, I pull back just enough to ask, "To what?"

"To show you how I feel about you," she whispers, silent

tears slipping down her cheeks. "You have to know by now."

Fuck yeah, I do. I'm just not sure I've done as good a job showing *her* what she means to me. I could've told her sooner—and maybe I should have—but tonight there's nothing in the world that could keep me from coming clean.

"That you love me?" I ask, smoothing the backs of my fingers against her cheek.

Her lips tremble as her eyes flutter shut, so much pinched emotion in her gorgeous face. "Yes," she rasps, and the greedy caveman inside of me beats his chest.

"Well, I happen to love you, too, so . . ."

Her eyes snap open again and I flash a grin.

"Maybe now you won't be so quick to question how I feel about *you*," I tease.

A low laugh starts in her belly, slowly making its way to her throat. "I don't know why I put up with you."

"Come on, babe . . . we both know it's because I'm a good fucking lay."

She slugs my arm and I swing her up off the ground, spinning us both around in the grass. She giggles and I'm positive I've never been this content . . . this *comfortable* in my own skin since I was a kid.

Somehow Kinsey has the ability to rile me in a way no one else can . . . and, just the same, she's the calming, reassuring force that keeps me grounded when I get too far inside my own head. I can't explain how or why she does what she does, but I love it.

I love *her*.

So goddamn much.

"How about we head inside and work off that cake?" I ask, carefully setting her down and snatching up her shoes. "I don't know if you noticed, but I had two pieces."

"So did I." Her grin is full of mischief. "On purpose."

I laugh again and she toes up and presses a kiss to my lips.

"I love you, Sergeant."

"I love you, too, princess."

ABOUT THE AUTHOR

MOLLY MCLAIN LIVES in a tiny Wisconsin town with her husband, three kids, and a sassy dog. She loves fountain soda, jellybeans, Luke Bryan and Avenged Sevenfold, thunderstorms, and camping at quiet lakes. She's been scribbling down love stories since she was old enough to dream about happily-ever-afters, and now she writes sexy, small town romance for real.

BOOKS BY
MOLLY McLAIN

The River Bend Series

Can't Shake You

Can't Hold Back

Can't Get Enough

Can't Walk Away

Can't Resist Him

Always Enough (short story)

A River Bend Wedding

The Velocity Series

Fly

Fight

ACKNOWLEDGEMENTS

THIS PART OF a book is perhaps one of the hardest to write, not because I can't think of anyone to thank . . . but because I can think of hundreds!

First and foremost, I have to thank Dana from Designs by Dana for taking my crazy idea one afternoon and turning it into a sexy as hell cover. More than that, thank you SO much for always being ready and willing to help me with every single thing I ask of you. Not even kidding when I say that you've made me teary with your awesomeness. Watch out for Vegas, chickie. I'mma bear hug the shit out of you!

Kristin, Kristin, Kristin . . . My PA and the girl who's always one step ahead of me. K, you cover my ass like a champ and, believe me, that's no small feat. You also put up with more of my OMG moments than you should have to. You, too, have been with me almost from the beginning and I hope you stick around. I wouldn't blame you if you didn't. I'm pretty fucking crazy. :D

Next, I have to thank my reader friends, the Misfits. I love you ladies so much! You are an endless support system that has never once let me down. You roll with me punches and cheer me on, no matter what kind of craziness I throw at you, and I can't thank you enough for that. I'm convinced you are the absolute BEST reader group out there and someday I'll find a way to show you properly.

Thanks so much to Ellie McLove for taking this project and dealing with my fangirl BS. I appreciate your thoughts and your time, and if you seriously want to be besties, I'll buy the charm bracelets. :D

To my beta readers, who I'm almost afraid to name in case I forget someone, but I'll try . . . Lisa, Andrea, Ashley, Amy, and Jessica, thank you so much for your honest thoughts on Trent and Kinsey. I appreciate your WTFs and your OMGs and your patience. Y'all are the best, and I'm happy to have you read for me anytime you want!

Last but certainly not least, I have to thank Christine from The Hype PR. Queenie, you're my rock. Sounds crazy, because we fuck around more than we probably get shit done, but I love your face. And your dick pics. :D